YOUNG ADULT FICTION BY BEVERLEY BOISSERY:

THE SOPHIE MALLORY SERIES

    Sophie's Rebellion
    Sophie's Treason
    Sophie's Exile

THE WAHMURRA SERIES

    The Convict's Thumbprint
    tHAD

THE PRIM HEIGHTS SERIES

    The 3Js

COMING NOVEMBER 2014

    Theo Bentley's War of 1812

tHAD

BEVERLEY BOISSERY

A WESBROOK BAY BOOKS PUBLICATION

2014

Copyright © 2013 Beverley Boissery

WESBROOK BAY BOOKS, VANCOUVER

All rights reserved.

ISBN-10:0987937677
ISBN-13:978-098-7937674

DEDICATION

This book is dedicated to The Arbutus Writers Group:

Mel Anastasiou
Paul O'Rourke
Susan Pieters
Kathy Tyers
Gordon Wilson.

With many thanks.

ACKNOWLEDGMENTS

The number of people to thank is amazing, primarily because the book took so long to be written. I'm very grateful to the early readers – such as The Arbutus Writers Group, Bron Short, Irena Tippett – who didn't like the original version. I know I've omitted names. Please forgive me.

I'm grateful to Dr. Timothy Hawkes and Mrs. Jenny Pearce of The King's School, Parramatta, N.S.W., Australia for their help and interest. King William's School is only very vaguely modelled after King's and is 99% a product of my imagination.

I'm grateful for the many holidays I spent as a child and young teen at Tahlee, my inspiration for Wahmurra. Its owner, Mr. White, listened to my stories, encouraged me to explore his extensive property, and gave me a beautiful fountain pen to put my words to paper. I don't think either of us ever dreamed that, eventually, they would be published. I'm grateful, as well, for the Theobalds who took over where Mr. White left off.

Katie Drysdale, Irena Tippett and Sam Friesen went over the manuscript with eagles' eyes. Chris Greenwood did his usual brilliant proofreading and plot-faulting. Thank you. The remaining idiocies are my responsibility.

Lastly, I'm grateful to each and every one of you who likes my writing, buys my books, and encourages me to continue. As Tiny Tim would say, "God Bless You."

BACKGROUND

tHAD is the sequel to *The Convict's Thumbprint*, published in 2011. In *The Convict's Thumbprint*, Chloe Murray searches for a special yellow brick that has the gouge of its convict maker's thumb. Once she puts her finger into the gouge, she travels back to the world of 1833.

Thad Compton's world. He was a thirteen year old who had stolen a gentleman's handkerchief in London, England. He had planned to sell it and buy food for his hungry siblings. Instead he was caught and sentenced to seven years in Australia.

After he survives the six months' voyage on a creaking sailing ship, he's assigned to Wahmurra, a huge estate about two hundred kilometers north of Sydney. The convict overseer is a brutal man called Ol' Bundy who comes to hate Thad.

Chloe and Thad become friends. Each of them is the best friend the other has ever had. So when the time comes for Chloe to go back to her home in the twenty-first century, she doesn't hesitate. She pulls Thad through the thumbprint with her and this book is the story of Thad's life in our century.

The story of his first five weeks can be found at the end of *The Convict's Thumbprint*. It's called *The Bridge*. I also put it up as a page on my website – http://www.beverleyboissery.com.

I hope you are surprised by what puzzles Thad the most about our century. It's not the technology. He was used to changes because of the Industrial Revolution. His big question: "What happened to God?" is a good one to think about.

1

SYDNEY. AUSTRALIA

I stared back at the shore of Double Bay. It was too dark to see much, but the first hints of dawn showed a man in the shadows. I let the rowboat rock in the waves, and hunkered down to eye level. An ultra-cautious move, probably unnecessary, because he felt safe enough to light a cigarette and, in the flare of the match, I saw his face.

Blimey!

Ol' Bundy terrified me and had for a very long time. Since 1833, in fact. My mates called him a right b*s*a*d. He was the convict overseer at a huge estate called Wahmurra, and I was a convict there. Neither of us belonged in the twenty-first century. But Chloe Murray had somehow pulled me through my own thumbprint in a special yellow brick, so here I was. And so, apparently, was Ol' Bundy.

When I tried to explain this to Chloe, her father and gran, they refused to listen. Mr. White, an ancient man who seemed to be my guardian, became frustrated. "Thaddeus Compton, listen to me. Listen hard. It is utterly impossible for Ol' Bundy to be here."

Well, of course, it was impossible.

I knew that. It was equally impossible for both of us. But Ol' Bundy was like a tracking dog where I was concerned. After Chloe dragged me into her twenty-first century world, it made perfect sense that Ol' Bundy found a way to follow me and make me miserable.

Until now I'd never had proof that he was here, and I needed something that Chloe and her family couldn't explain away. I looked back at the man with the cigarette. Well, now they had it. All they had to do was look out their windows.

I let the rowboat drift a little more as I thought. Finally, I dialed 000, the emergency number. A voice answered immediately. "Good morning, what's your emergency?"

"There's a man outside my house, and he's, um, sort of…" I stopped, hoping the woman would understand.

No such luck. "You have to give me more details."

"Well, he keeps…" I didn't want to tell an outright lie, but the chance to catch Ol' Bundy was too good to pass up. "Er, his trousers. He keeps…"

"You mean he's exposing himself? What's your address?"

I felt the slightest bit guilty as I rattled off Gran's address.

"I'll dispatch a car immediately."

Gotcha, matey, I smirked and ended the call. I didn't want to get into any further details and I lay in the boat until I saw flashing lights come down the road towards Gran's house. As soon as they stopped, I picked up my oars and started powering my way toward Darling Point.

Near-dawn was always perfect. It was the only time I could still be myself. I stopped rowing for a moment and looked back at Double Bay, imagining it the way it looked back in 1833. It had been incredibly beautiful then with flowering trees right down to the shoreline. If I looked hard I'd have seen a native fisherman, standing on one leg as he peered into the water, waiting for an unwary fish to come by. Now, houses competed for space with tall buildings like commuters on the buses.

I picked up the oars again and headed off in the direction of the Opera House and was halfway there when my phone rang. Chloe, of course. She had this gigantic protective thing towards me. Usually I appreciated it. But I wanted to see the look on her face when I told her I'd caught Ol' Bundy so I didn't bother taking it out of my pocket.

The phone went again. I thought about Chloe's tenacity, knew she'd keep texting, so I pulled it out and looked at the screen.

HOME.

Yeah, yeah. I turned the opposite way and rowed towards Clark Island as though I were racing in the Olympics. Once more, my phone rang and, after I'd circled the island, I looked at it again.

HOME. NOW. HOME!!! NOW!!! HOME!!!!

This wasn't normal even for Chloe. Was I in trouble because of the trick on Ol' Bundy?

This time I powered up as though I were racing neck and neck with an American and I could see the finish line. As I rounded Darling Point I looked up and saw Chloe dancing on Gran's wharf impatiently. She waved, so I knew there wouldn't be another text. At least, not for another minute.

She helped me tie up the rowboat. Tell the truth, I was grateful because I was pretty well knackered. As soon as I pulled my sweater over my head, she started talking. "Thad, you're impossible. But I don't have time for that now because something huge has happened. Don't know what. I haven't seen Dad look this angry for four years, and Gran is up and making breakfast. Dad said to get you back because we have to talk."

When we walked into the kitchen Gran pushed plates of food at us, and I thought I saw her brush a tear away. Mr. Murray just glowered at his mobile, willing it to ring. It seemed anti-climatic when I heard a motorbike snarl its way down Gran's driveway. Mr. Murray was already moving when we heard the thuds of someone knocking at the front door. I followed, and stood stockstill when I saw the bike's rider.

It was instant lust. For his jacket. It was made of a shiny black leather and a fancy gold zipper went from neck to waist. I'd never seen anything quite like it and was only brought back to earth when Chloe giggled.

"If you've ever wondered, not that I think you would, but if you've ever wondered if you're male, you've just had your answer. Black leather jackets and males go together like…"

"Like get back into the kitchen. We need to talk," Mr. Murray interrupted. The messenger handed over a packet and, as we walked into the kitchen, I heard the bike's roar as it climbed back up the hill.

Mr. Murray looked even grimmer when he opened the package, pulled out four copies of a newspaper, and handed one to each of us. "This morning's edition."

I grinned when I saw what it was. *Gotta Know* was Sydney's least respected newspaper. Gran called it pig's swill. I'd never read pig's swill so I opened it up to find out what it was.

Jaw dropping--that's what it was. There was a naked woman on page three with breasts as huge as inverted moon craters, and I could almost feel my jaw hit the floor and a blush work its way up from my neck.

"Get your mind out of the gutter. Look at the front page," Chloe said and poked me hard.

When I turned back to the page, I understood everything. Mr. Murray's grimness, Gran's tears and Chloe's anger, because the headline screamed, *"CHRISTINA MURRAY ALIVE!"*

Christina Murray was Chloe's mom, and a fuzzy picture of a body in a hospital bed took up half of *Gotta Know's* front page. Underneath was a rehash of stories written four years earlier when she had disappeared. An arrow directed readers to page 7.

There were more pictures there. Better ones in focus. One showed an incredibly ancient man, surrounded by tall men with huge muscles, entering Greenway Hospital. It was Mr. White, and the newspaper wondered who else could have brought him to Greenway but Christina Murray. Another picture showed Gran and Chloe leaving the hospital, and both seemed to be crying. The last photo was a picture of Mr. Murray at the premiere of one of his movies in Los Angeles.

Obediently I turned to the front page again and studied the fuzzy picture. "Look!" I pointed to the body's crooked leg. "It's me. Someone took a picture of me."

"So now you know why we've been so careful about you," she answered.

"And why we panic when you row off in that boat of yours," her father added.

I heard a quiet sob and turned towards Gran. I really loved her. I'd never had a grandmother, and she was everything I thought one would be like. She'd done little things for me, like taking me to get my thatch of black hair tamed properly and found me fun clothes to wear.

"It's so unfair," she said quietly. "It's like losing her again when I'd just begun to feel happy about everything." There was an angry anguish in her voice when she added, "Why don't we tell them the truth? Why not say that we know she's dead, because if she were alive she'd find a way to let us know that she was well and happy?" She stopped, thought for a moment, and a tiny smile appeared. "We just don't say that she has. Communicated, that is."

Mr. Murray shook his head. "It's none of their business. I want to…."

Before he could finish, his mobile rang, and he listened for a long time. "That was Mr. White," he said eventually. "He's called a media conference for nine o'clock and suggests that Chloe and Thad go to Wahmurra. He's sending a car in an hour. Gran and I will 'copter up afterwards."

Gran crossed her arms, and ordinarily I would have grinned. "If he thinks I'm allowing myself to go into a helicopter, he has another think coming. And, I am definitely not going to Wahmurra. You know what I think of that benighted place."

Mr. Murray ran his hand through his hair. "Well, you can't stay here. The paparazzi's on its way. You'll be stalked everywhere."

"Humph. Jane Kuizinas is always inviting me to stay with her. It's the right time now. Nobody will look for me in Vancouver."

Mr. Murray nodded. "Get the afternoon flight. Well, that's it. Everything's settled." He stood up and then turned back, as if he'd remembered something. "Oh, one more thing. Thad, Mr. White said the story's byline might help your nightmares, and that he'd had an interesting conversation with the police this morning."

I blushed, then looked at the byline. When I read frank.bundy@gottaknow.com.au, I didn't know what to think. I'd been in the twenty-first century for about six weeks, and four of those had been in Greenway. How had

Ol' Bundy been here long enough to get a job? "I don't understand," I told Mr. Murray. "I don't think Frank's his right name, but I guess the police would know."

"Know what?"

After I told them what I'd done, they laughed. "So that's what Mr. White meant by the police," Mr. Murray said. "But Thad, get it through your head. Frank Bundy might look exactly like his ancestor, but that's all it is."

I couldn't accept it. "Nobody has that hair color. I swear, Mr. Murray, Ol' Bundy's got here somehow."

Gran walked across and put her hand on my head. Although it was a loving touch, her voice was annoyed. "You're being stupid, Thad, and I'm sick of it. It's genes. If this Frank Bundy took those pictures, then I figure you saw him. I believe too that he's descended from your Bundy, hair color and all. Some families reproduce the same face and hair color over and over through the generations. Chloe looks exactly as I did at her age. If you would like to see them, I can bring out the photos and show you Chloe's baby pictures and mine."

"We don't have time, and I'm so grateful for that," Chloe interrupted. She pushed her chair back, and put her dishes into the dishwasher. "Come on, Thad. Get your act together. We've got packing to do. We're going to Wahmurra."

2

As Mr. White's Rolls sped its way along the F3 towards Wahmurra, I found myself mildly disappointed. Everyone had emphasized how important he was, apparently one of the most powerful men in Australia. Yet, the car looked like an antique.

Chloe and I sat in the back seat. A glass window separated us from the driver. Below the glass was a wonderful wall of tiny cupboards—one held whisky and brandy, not that we were allowed to touch them. My seat was leather. It felt amazingly comfortable but also like sitting on a moving armchair.

In the old days, I used to ride a horse every day and I developed a relationship with it. We trusted each other. I had to trust that the horse would jump a fence when I asked, and it had to trust that I wouldn't make it try something impossible.

Mr. White's moving armchair offered nothing but comfort. It was boring, but so was the scenery. Towering office towers no longer fascinated me. Sadly, it had only taken six weeks for the wonder of them to disappear, and I had no real sense of where we were. When I'd ridden down to Sydney from Wahmurra, I'd sort of known every tree along the way. Surrounded by neat rows of houses and forests of office towers, I was lost.

I leaned back against the soft leather and brooded myself into a nap. Chloe's elbow in my ribs jerked me awake. "Look, Thad. Dubbees!"

When I looked where she was pointing, I saw the Hawkesbury River. "Dubbees?"

"Look!"

I followed the direction of her finger and saw, far below, an elongated boat with eight rowers. They sped under the bridge, their maroon and green-tipped oars leaving perfect shell-like hollows in the river. "Dubbing? Is that what you call rowing?"

Chloe laughed. "Stupid. It's just that King William's boys always have nicknames. We call them Dubbees, but Dad said he was called a Billy and in his father's time it was Billy-goats."

The twenty-first century seemed full of things I both looked forward to and was scared by. King William's School for Boys was one of those. I'd be going there once I'd had the operation to get my leg fixed. In my proper time, it was a school for boys like Billy Kendricks. Yet I'd once told Chloe that I wanted to learn more than anything else. Being called a Dubbee maybe wasn't that high a price if I got to go to the school.

The Hawkesbury was the last thing I recognized for a long time. Entire cities had been built where there had once been only bush, and I started worrying again about Wahmurra. Would I still recognize it?

Again Chloe interrupted my thoughts. "Any second now." Then, as the car turned off the highway, she leaned back in her seat. "We're here. Only twenty more minutes. We're on Wahmurra land now. Nearly home."

Home? Where, when was home? Then I recognized something and had my answer. The orange dirt road was twice as wide as it had once been, but it was the way to

Wahmurra and Wahmurra was home. It was incredible. A hot-cross bun kind of feeling. Almost immediately, I saw more and more things I recognized.

"There's Grady's Hill," I told Chloe, jumping up and almost hitting the roof of the car in my excitement. "And look. Over there. It's Paddy's Pond."

Thirty kangaroos ringed the waterhole and they lifted their heads, as though saying hello, when we drove by. "Must be tea time," Chloe commented. "Now, look out my side. You can just see the church."

The church.

Although I'd never seen it before, it had precipitated everything, but once we got closer I felt disappointed. Up to that moment, I wouldn't have been able to say what I expected, but now I knew. Given its power on me and the Murray family, I expected to see something magnificent like St. Paul's Cathedral in London, or, at a minimum, the flying buttresses of Westminster Abbey.

Wahmurra's convicts, men I'd once known, had carried stones from the fields and creeks to build the small church's walls. Instead of a lofty dome or spire, its roof was tin. It was very small. Maybe fifty people could jam into it. Yet when Chloe's mother had touched one of its pews, she'd sent my world and hers seriously out of kilter.

Then the car stopped, and Chloe screamed the obvious, "We're here."

I got out of the car slowly and on the wrong side, so that I faced the headlands to Port Adams. Needing more time, and lots more courage, I walked across to an old cannon. It still pointed towards the port's entrance, but it had been painted over so many times since it had once guarded against French warships that I doubted it could still shoot anything.

When I looked down at the water, I saw a mess of rotting posts; all that remained of the bustling wharf complex of my time. Further along the shoreline was a marina with sleek state-of-the-art yachts and power boats.

"Has it changed so much?" Chloe asked softly.

I'd been too preoccupied to hear her approach. "Maybe."

She gave me a fast hug and, deciding to face my fears, I turned around. Right in front of me was an old building called the Barracks. At this time of day in 1833, soldiers would be climbing its stairs and going to their rooms to change into dinner dress uniforms before heading for the mess hall. Servants would scurry around bringing hot water for their baths. Cows would be bellowing as they waited to be milked, and there'd be noise everywhere as day workers and convicts finished their day's work.

Mr. White had turned it into a high-priced retreat for executives with its own spa, a communications tower, helicopter pad, and a high-priced chef who produced fantastic meals in its Bistro. "You'll recognize the Bistro. It's the old officers' mess hall," Chloe assured me.

She was half-right. Instead of the hubble and bubble of officers ending their day, there was a relative silence except, that is, for a jet screaming overhead as it climbed for altitude. A group of riders cantered up the hill and then headed for the stables. Down in the marina seagulls squabbled over something—probably someone's catch of the day.

The huge difference was that everything looked so clean and so well looked after. The army's old parade ground now looked as though a gardener cut it with scissors. Flanked by jacaranda and flame trees, purple and red bougainvillea trailed over a couple of trellises. Even the driveway had white pebbles on it, and the posts along it looked like they'd been painted that very morning.

So far, so good. I slowly pivoted until I faced the heart of Wahmurra—the oldest building, the House—and I felt a long sigh let out all my anxiety. It hadn't really changed. If I closed my eyes I could easily imagine five-year-old Polly Kendricks running towards me with her dress torn and stained, and Billy, her twin, protesting at the top of his voice that he wasn't to blame. It seemed so real that I smiled as I walked across over to the House.

Mr. White stood by the open front door, "Welcome home, Thad, though I suppose I should say, welcome back."

I teared up, especially when Mr. White's frail arms crept around me in what amounted to a hug. I wanted to put my head on his bony shoulders and tell him my fears and frustrations with the twenty-first century.

But, I couldn't. The man hugging me was so similar, yet so different from my Mr. White of the 1830s. That Mr. White had been young and dynamic enough to rule over three hundred convicts. I hadn't really trusted him, and the big difference between him and the present Mr. White was that I wanted to love this twenty-first century one.

Mr. Murray appeared out of nowhere with my backpack. "Hang in there, Thad. You look worn out. Have a rest. Just make sure you leave enough time to change your clothes for dinner. Mr. White's taking us over to the Bistro tonight."

Chloe came with my other pack and kissed Mr. White's cheek. "Thanks for having us." Then she grabbed my hand, "Come on, Thad. Let's get you settled."

Mr. White led the way, and when he stopped in front of a bedroom, Chloe giggled. In 1833, it had been Billy's room. After Mr. White left, she helped put my clothes into drawers and arrange my toothbrush and stuff in the bathroom. I tried to help, but I was concentrating on not looking over my shoulder. Ghosts seemed everywhere.

Just before leaving, Chloe threw my young James Bond book onto the bed. "Dad's right, Thad. You do look pale. Have a bath, a rest. Whatever. But just make sure that when the second gong sounds, you're in your good clothes and walking towards the Bistro. Mr. White is very formal and insists on punctuality."

"Yeah, yeah."

Too exhausted to think, I threw myself onto the bed. I tried to read, but it was useless. Billy's room had always been shadier than the others, because it was paneled with red cedar. But Chloe had pushed the curtains open, and light from the setting sun bathed one corner and, just before my eyes closed, I saw something carved near the ceiling:

tHAD

I would have bet that the day could not have become more emotional, but it just had. I fought back tears as I climbed a chair and traced the letters and the arrow with my fingers. I knew, without doubt, that Billy had carved them because of the small 't' beginning Thad. Even though he was only five, Billy had started lessons and had obstinately written my name like that.

I wondered for a minute what the arrow meant, then

I started manhandling a chest of drawers away from the wall. When I looked, there was absolutely nothing. I went back to the top and started tracing my way down but, no matter how hard I looked, I couldn't find a thing. I needed better light to hunt properly.

Then the second gong sounded. I looked down at myself. My hands, shorts, and shirts were filthy, and I could hear Chloe's warning about clothes and punctuality as clear as a bell. Muttering words that probably hadn't been heard in the House since its convict days, I scrambled into my dress pants and shirt and grabbed my jacket and tie.

I wasn't fast enough. Mr. Murray stood outside the door, his face grim. He snatched the tie out of my hand and pulled it over my head. "Chloe's already gone across with Mr. White," he announced as he began manipulating both ends of the tie in a knot. "You've really got to learn this, Thad. You'll have to do it every day at school. Now, watch. You take the narrow end and, abracadabra, a perfectly knotted tie."

Who had invented ties? I grumbled about them all the way across to the Bistro and then sneered at Chloe's spinach salad. "That's the stuff we used to feed the chooks."

"Chickens, not chooks," she corrected in her best grown up voice. Then she reverted to normal and said, "Anyway, you can't talk. You're nothing but a carnivore."

"No, I'm not." I thought of my new favorite food. Balmain Bugs were a type of lobster and far outclassed the steak I was currently devouring. "I'm…." I broke off and searched my vocabulary. "I'm an omnivore."

"Prove it." Chloe challenged and pushed her salad across the table.

We went at each other back and forth until Mr. White intervened. "Enough. You two sound like Billy and Polly."

"Like Billy and Polly?"

I knew I sounded incredulous. That's because I was. I turned to Mr. White, "How do *you* know what they sounded like?"

Strangely enough, he seemed to blush before adroitly changing the topic. He leaned towards Mr. Murray and asked, "Zach? When might we expect your Mr. Dellman?"

"Wednesday. He's on the early flight out of Los Angeles. Once he lands, he'll take the 'copter up here. Expect him for lunch?"

Determined to find out about Billy and Polly, I repeated my question: "How do you know what Billy and Polly sounded like?"

"Who's Mr. Dellmann?" Chloe asked at the same time.

"The best voice coach I know," her father answered. "Thad's accent will raise a lot of eyebrows. And questions. Particularly at school, so I asked Tyce to give him a vaguely mid-Pacific accent."

"Mid-Pacific? Why not Australian?"

"Foreigners are allowed to make mistakes. If people think Thad's lived here all his life, they'll expect him to know everything. If he doesn't, it will be like a red flag. But if they think he's just moved here and doesn't know any better, they'll shrug. It's for his protection."

I'd still been thinking about Mr. White and Billy and Polly until half-way through Mr. Murray's explanation. Once I clued in, I didn't know what to think. Of course I sounded different. Like I said "wot" instead of "what." But why mid-Pacific, whatever that was?

And, whatever it was, it sounded suspiciously like school. I gloomed quietly while eating my passion fruit sundae, trying to figure out who I wanted to question most, when Chloe kicked me under the table and asked, "Dad? If you and Mr. White are going to drink brandy, may we be excused?"

We walked towards the headland. I kept silent. Too silent because Chloe suddenly asked, "What's the matter, Thad?"

"I'm thinking."

"About?"

About Billy, what the arrow pointed to, and if he's in the church's graveyard. "About mid-Pacific accents," I said instead. "What's the matter with the way I speak?"

"You mean wot's the matter wif the waiy you tork?" When I didn't smile, she went on quickly, "Thad, nobody speaks like that nowadays. Dad's right. You'll stand out, and the whole thing is to get you to blend in."

We stopped at the cannon and I lifted one of the cannonballs. It was shiny black, and I held it high so that Chloe could see it. "Don't you understand? This should be rusty by now. But it's been painted so many times to make it look pretty that I don't think it would fit into the gun's barrel anymore. See? It's not really a cannonball anymore because it can't do its proper job. It's just a chunk of iron."

Chloe took the cannonball and tried to fit it into the cannon's barrel. "You're right. I think it's a good job we no longer rely on this," she said, cradling the old ball and looking out to sea. "But, Thad, painted cannonballs aren't the problem, are they? What's really worrying you?"

I walked until I was almost on the edge of the cliff. "I don't know. I think I've accepted that I'm really here, but I can't help wondering where I'd end up if I just stepped off. Your century? Mine? Heaven?"

She pulled me back a step or two. "Well, you're not going to jump, so the answer is my century, Thad. The twenty-first. Face it. You're here."

I shook her off and defiantly walked back to where I'd

been. "I keep looking for ships with three masts to come through the headlands, Chloe, but there's only these fancy yachts. When we ate dinner, I half-expected Major Barney to storm through the door and get me flogged for being in the wrong place."

I bent down and worked at a piece of grass so that she couldn't see my face. "Chloe, I'm gutted. All the people I knew and loved, like Billy, even those I detested, like Ol' Bundy, are probably in the graveyard behind the church."

She looked sympathetic, and it added to my anger. "Don't you get it? Mr. White and Dr. Mansfield keep telling me that after the operation, I'll run as fast as I used to. Now, your father's arranged for some voice coach to make me sound proper. It's too much. I feel I'm like the cannonball being painted and repainted until there's nothing left of me. What will happen then?"

Chloe pulled me back again and this time held me tightly. "All the changes are really superficial, Thad. The operation's maybe a big deal, but so what? Everything else is just camouflage—the great haircut, the accent change, the way you'll walk. The things that make you you—your courage, your sense of honor—they'll still be there underneath the mid-Pacific accent. Fundamentals don't change."

I shook her off again. This time, I was furious and I know my voice sounded bitter when I turned on her. "Fundamentals? You want to talk about fundamentals? Then, tell me this. What's happened to God? He used to be the center of everything, and I learned to love him with my heart, soul, and spirit. Now? He's some sort of periphery in your century. Your dad calls this a post-Christian world. I know God doesn't ever stop loving us. Why did your people stop loving Him? What happened?"

Chloe looked astonished. "We still do. Love him, that is.

Well, if I'm going to be honest, some of us do. Anyway, I go to chapel twice a week at school and every Sunday night. You'll have to as well, once you start at King William's."

"Big deal," I mocked. "Going to church doesn't mean anything. I went to the zoo, but it didn't make me a kangaroo." I started walking away and when she followed, I turned around again. "I don't want to talk about this anymore. I'm going to try to find the old chapel and I'm going to pray. By myself. You're not welcome."

3

I woke up the next morning determined to find what the arrow pointed to. I needed to do something to stop myself thinking. Changing the way I spoke wasn't camouflage to me. My mam had made me say my prayers every night. It was from them that I'd learned to talk. It wasn't educated or high class, but the way I spoke was the last thing I had left from 1833 and from my mam. That is, until I found what Billy had left for me.

After breakfast I went straight to my bedroom and started manhandling the furniture again. I searched the paneled wall from top to bottom and eventually sat down in total disgust. Billy's directions seemed so clear. The arrow didn't point to the other walls. I got ready to search all over again when Chloe knocked on the door.

"Let me in. I know you're feeling sorry for yourself."

I let her go on for a few minutes before succumbing. If I hadn't, she would have knocked until lunch time and, the truth was, I was getting nowhere. I showed her the arrow, and she just about screamed the house down. I thought about telling her that the message was for me, not her, but she was already all in, down on her belly, peering and tapping at the wall.

I climbed back onto the chair when she said, "Thad, get down and come here. See how these boards are smaller. I bet there's a tiny cupboard behind them."

I lost my sulkiness when I tapped the boards she

pointed to and felt them move. Both of us had to push hard until finally the door collapsed and we saw a cavity. I reached in and pulled a dusty package from its hiding place. I got off my knees, sat on the bed, and dusted the package off. For a while I simply sat, cradling the package, tears running down my face.

Billy hadn't forgotten me. He cared enough to communicate.

"It's from Billy," I said unnecessarily while my fingers picked at the knots in a dusty old tie Billy had used instead of string. Finally I got the wrappings off and held up four pages of creased faded paper.

"That's it?"

I thought the same. It seemed a lot of trouble for just four pages. Furthermore, I could only read one of them. Chloe crammed her body close so that she could see them as well. "This looks like some crazy foreign language."

The paper was old and fragile and the ink had faded. Nevertheless it was still fragile. "This one's ancient Greek, though I have no idea what the others are."

"Well? Go on. What does this one say?"

I felt her body tense as I took my time deciphering the letter. Just before she exploded on me, I said, "It's from Billy. Basically he hopes I'm doing well and he wants me to know that he's left a few other packages around, in case I don't find this. Plus, there's more letters and photographs in King William's library waiting for me. I have no idea how he knew I'd go there."

"Mom," Chloe said immediately. "She'd have figured it out. Now, what about the others."

"Okay. Here's the second one."

A	*N*
BILLY	*OVYYL*
THAD	*GUNQ*

tHAD

> ?   *YRBANEQB QN IVAPV*
> ?   *GUVAX UNEQ, GUNQ*

She looked at the page, then snorted in disgust. "We're expected to read this?"

"I am anyway," I said, though I wondered if I could.

Our mobiles pinged simultaneously. When I looked down Mr. Murray had texted, "Barracks. Now."

I got up and started maneuvering the chest of drawers back against the wall. "Give me a hand, will you?" I asked, and when Chloe didn't come to help I looked back to the bed. She still sat on it, but her face looked like it had lost two shades of tan. "What's wrong?"

"Tell you later. Got to check something first."

She jumped to her feet with the old tie Billy had used for string in her hands. She looked like she'd been poleaxed and, even though she helped push the chest back in place, she shuddered when she put the tie in her back pocket.

Even outside in the sunshine, she still looked as though she'd had a gigantic shock. "What's the matter?" I kept asking.

"Later," she insisted. "There's Dad. Let's find out what he wants."

Our company for the day, it turned out. He'd booked us into a dolphin watching cruise and organized kayaking. He seemed disappointed by our lack of enthusiasm. "What's wrong?"

"It sounds great," I started and then looked at Chloe. "It's just that we wanted to do something else this morning. Can we kayak and dolphin watch tomorrow? Please?"

"I suppose so." Mr. Murray pulled out his phone. "Just let me cancel so I don't lose the deposit, then I want to know what's got you so all-fired busy. You probably don't want to tell me about it, but you have a minute to work out which one of you does."

From the way he looked at us, I knew he was working out which of us he could pressure. It would be me, of course. Chloe had years of practice in keeping secrets from him. Sure enough, when I didn't answer immediately, he said, "Okay, Thad. Spill the beans."

"It's a puzzle, sir. Do you know anything about codes?"

It was exactly the right question. He looked interested when he said, "A little. One of my movies involved a couple of codes a few years ago, so I did enough research to make sure we weren't going to look stupid. Why, Thad? Have you found one?"

"Well, we found an old letter, but we can't work out what's on it." I looked at Chloe who nodded. "Sir, will you help us?"

"It might be easier if we go to the Barracks' library. Where is this letter?"

"I'll go and get it," Chloe volunteered. "Meet you there."

After we settled, I realized that Mr. Murray did indeed know about codes. When he explained that an "alphabet substitution" was the easiest form of code, I breathed in relief. "So what you're telling us is that we make two list A-M and N-Z, right?"

"Like this," Mr. Murray said as he ripped a sheet off a writing pad and folded it in half lengthwise. He wrote A then B underneath it and quickly filled in the rest of the alphabet:

A B C D E F G H I J K L M
N O P Q R S T U V W X Y Z

"That's brilliant," Chloe said. "You just substitute the letter opposite the one you want to write. So the first letter of Thad's name would be G…"

"And then UNQ," her father interrupted.

Chloe laughed. "Thad's a gunq, Thad's a gunq."

"Okay, okay, Chloe. I get it," I interrupted because, if I hadn't, she would have gone on forever.

Mr. Murray looked at us and then back at me. "Are either of you going to tell me what this is about."

Chloe intervened. "Later, Dad. And, maybe." Before he could object, she pulled the old tie from her pocket. "Dad, this is a King William's tie, isn't it?"

Mr. Murray sat up with a jerk. He looked at the dirty maroon and green tie for the longest time and then at us. "I don't know what your secret is, but I'm prepared to wait. But this?" He broke off and pointed to the tie. "This I want to know about immediately. Like, how on earth you managed to come across it."

I couldn't understand his reaction. "We found it in my bedroom."

"It is a King William's tie though, isn't it?" Chloe asked.

Her father picked it up. "It is indeed. It's supposed to be a secret until the first school assembly ten days from now. The boxes are locked in the school store and, until that assembly, no one will have this tie."

Chloe's face showed the shock I felt. "So you're saying they haven't been sold yet?"

"That's exactly what I'm saying. Not sold, not distributed, not handed out. The boxes arrived last week and won't be touched until next week. Now, Chloe, speaking as one of the board of governors, I want to know where you found it and why it is so dirty."

"Like Thad said. We found it in his room."

Mr. Murray picked up the tie again. "It's definitely the new one, all right. We've changed suppliers, and this is the new supplier's label. I suppose someone from the design committee must have stayed here and mislaid it. Careless idiot."

"Mislaid, of course," Chloe said in a neutral kind of voice.

I didn't have a voice, neutral or otherwise. I now understood Chloe's shock when she'd first seen the tie. I had no idea why or when it had been wrapped around Billy's letter. But one thing I knew, and I knew it for sure.

Billy Kendricks hadn't been a member of this year's tie design committee.

4

Before an awkward silence developed, Mr. Murray's phone rang. He checked the ID, pulled a face and excused himself.

I looked at Chloe. "Okay. Let's get working."

For once she didn't argue or try to boss me around. She just pulled the writing pad towards her and smiled, "So Gunq, you read the letter from Billy's message out. I'll decode it and write it down."

"Right. Here we go—W R B."

As we kept going, Billy's message became obvious.

Leonardo da Vinci. Think hard, Thad.

"What do you think he means, Thad? What are you supposed to think hard about?"

I ran my fingers through my hair. I didn't know what I expected, but it certainly wasn't this. Billy Kendricks knowing about da Vinci? I hadn't a clue when I'd seen the Mona Lisa's face on a commercial and asked Mr. Murray about her. "I have no idea," I told Chloe and shrugged. "Even worse, this was supposed to be the easiest clue." I pushed another sheet of paper across for Chloe to study.

Its message had seemed simple when I'd first glanced across as it. But when she took it, my fingers somehow stuck to the paper, or maybe she pulled too impatiently. Whatever. The end result was that we ripped the sheet into two. Before she could say anything, I put the two bits together (sort of) and beckoned her over. "Now, what do you think it means?"

On one half of the rip was a backward looking half circle or a C written back to front, and on the other bit:

III bɘɘя

"I think Billy wrote beer. He always refused to use a capital letter to begin a word."

Chloe nodded. "I remember. I was cHLOE. Maybe he was dyslexic or something. But, it doesn't really help, does it? Three beer? Three beer and a circle? Three half circle beers?"

I shrugged and unfolded the last two sheets of Billy's message. "I don't know. But this is the message I think it's supposed to unlock."

The sheets weren't gibberish—but they might have well as been:

8 | 99, 70, 1 | 188, 92, 26 | 227, 33, 107, 93 | 10, 8, 43, 12, 93. | 213, 79, 116 | 1, 61, 272, 20 | 131 | 272, 20, 22 | 100, 10, 55 | 43, 272, 19, 20, 54 | 4, 7, 272, 8, 257, 256, 28 | 118, 15, 12, 63, 67, 227 | J, 131, 15, 23, 95, 80. | 188, 86, 116 | 223, 21, 21, 23, 20, 22 | 29, 6, 31, 62, 213.

93, 112, 71, 28 | 93, 112, 95, 272, 256 | 105, 4 | 97, 92, 272, 95 | 93, 112, 255, 50 | 21, 54, 95 | 1, 6, 188 | 3, 95, 93, 27, 256, 20, 54 | 67, 26, 272 | 17, 72, 272, 223, 28, 84. | 227, 21, 42, 23 | 241, 32, 29, 9, 50, 22 | 7, 12, 19 | 18, 103, 102, 111, 112 | 99, 96, 86, 54, 256 | 102, 272, 21, 97 | 7, 12, 19 | 115, 235, 86, 82, 272 | 9, 50 | 7, 12, 19 | 5, 92, 92, 93 | 112, 92, 116, 4, 19 | 110, 54 | 28, 79, 116, 3, 235, 19 | 241, 46, 213.

3, 8, 227, 235, 213

Chloe looked at the two pages of numbers. "I think we need Dad again. Let's copy these out for ourselves. Billy's originals are too fragile to be worked on. We should probably make a couple of spares as well." She took photos of them with her phone, and then we started doing things the old-fashioned way with pencils and paper.

After lunch she pulled one of the copies from her pocket and handed it to her father. "Can you help us, Dad? Do you know what this is?"

"Short answer? A headache."

"Why?"

Mr. Murray studied the sheets. "From the little I know, I'd say this was a book cipher. Each number is the first letter of a word in a certain page of a book. You have to know which book it is before you can do anything, so whoever wrote this should have also told you its title. Did they?"

After we shook our heads, Mr. Murray looked at the numbers again. "There's one more possibility. People sometimes use long documents instead of books. Like the Magna Carta or Lincoln's Gettysburg Address. Something that's long but not too hard to find."

I frowned. I understood. "But what you're saying is that it doesn't matter whether it's a book or something long. Unless we know what it is, we can't do anything. Right?"

Mr. Murray nodded and sipped his coffee. Now, *quid pro quo*. I told you what I know, you tell me what it's about."

Chloe looked at me and she seemed as glum as I felt. Billy had given us clues, but they made no sense. What did Leonardo da Vinci have to do with three beers? I wanted to go back to the library, but Mr. Murray had other ideas.

"These are the last days of your summer holidays, and I will not allow you to obsess over numbers, however puzzling, indoors. I have the boat ready, and you have five minutes to be on it. And Thad, don't forget your sunscreen."

Sunscreen? I would have been scorned to bits if anyone from the old days had seen me put it on. I was used to working outdoors every day for fourteen hours. It hadn't hurt me then, and I couldn't understand why I had to wear sunscreen now. But it was an argument I never won, so I obediently went to my room and slathered myself in it.

We weren't allowed to work on codes the following day either. At first I rebelled, but then I rediscovered the rhythms of my Wahmurra days. Up at the crack of dawn to row on the still water of Port Adams and I once talked Mr. Murray into letting me show him the famous current off Oyster Creek that zapped a boat almost to the middle of the harbor in seconds.

Afternoons were lazy times. We swam in Lady's Cove or kayaked. One day we took a picnic lunch and rode on Wahmurra's horses to a tiny glade with its own waterfall. When I saw it still unspoiled after two centuries, I could have danced with delight. My most secret place was still intact. I still had a hide out if I needed one, because there was a little cave behind the waterfall. No one, except me, had ever found it.

Finally Mr. Murray brought up the topic of the numbers puzzle. "I should have pointed something out. Can you show me the sheets again?" I ran to my bedroom and when I brought them back, Mr. Murray studied them. "Right. I did remember properly. In the second paragraph, there's a little repetition. 7, 12, 19. See? I think that means "the." If so the last word of the message ends in an e."

That made sense. "And I think the very last bit is Billy's name."

"It can't be," Chloe interrupted. We'd had this argument several times. "There are two ll's in Billy and that word doesn't have two numbers the same."

"It's a long document and lots of words might begin with 'l'," Mr. Murray said and went to join Mr. White on the balcony.

Tyce Dellman arrived the next day and there went our unstructured time. He loved sailing, so we spent the mornings out on the water in Wahmurra's catamaran and gradually we learned what he did for a living.

"I specialize in old English accents," he said. "Any time there's a historical movie or somebody's doing Shakespeare, they call me in to get the accents half between what they should be and what we'll understand."

"Could you make me sound like I was born in 1830?" Chloe asked.

Tyce looked at her. "Probably, but I could guarantee one hundred percent success with Thad, here."

I scowled and deliberately turned the cat into a yacht's wake so Tyce had to scramble to avoid the spray.

Chloe took me to task later when we sat on Lady Cove's beach. "That was mean. He's kind of an ish. I think he'll look after you."

"An ish?"

She shrugged. "You know. Stylish, youngish, dish-ish."

I nodded. Tyce was one of those people who never seemed to have a hair out of place. His clothes were subtly different from everyone's, even Mr. Murray. I'd seen faces like his in magazines when Gran took me to get my hair cut. "Well, one thing. He's definitely not ugly-ish. He's too perfect, if anything. He makes me feel like I'm a museum sometimes. I'll say something, and he takes his notebook out. Your dad's convinced him that I was kidnapped. He keeps trying to find out about that without 'traumatizing' me. It's like a game I play with him."

Chloe stood up and wrapped her towel around her. "Well, just make sure you keep winning that particular game. He doesn't need to know more about you, and he certainly doesn't need to know that your accent's the real deal. You just keep remembering why everything about you is a secret."

Mr. White found out my deepest secret, though. After everyone was asleep, I usually went across to the space beneath the Barracks' stairs. I'd find the yellow brick and push my thumb into the dent it had made in the brick so long ago. I wasn't quite sure what I'd do if anything happened, but I needed to find out if I could get back to 1833 if life became unbearable.

"Doesn't work, does it?"

Mr. White's whispery voice startled me so much that my head hit the rafters. "Ouch. That hurt."

Mr. White ignored my protest and pointed to the yellow brick. "The gouge won't work for you. I know, because I've tried it so many times."

Talk about atomic-sized shocks? Mr. White wanted to go to another time-world? It didn't seem possible at his age.

He hadn't finished talking though. "What are you hoping for, Thad? If you touch the brick and saw both worlds at once, which one would you choose?"

"I've promised you that I'll stay here for a year." I knew I sounded sulky, but I felt sulky. I wondered if I could make Mr. White understand my desperation for a bolt-hole. "Ever since I was arrested in London, I've always found some place to escape to if I couldn't handle things. I need that escape-hatch, sir. I really do."

Mr. White took his time before he said anything. He took a cigar from his pocket and did all the fiddly things cigar-smokers do before they light up. He turned away, and I was glad. I hated the smell of cigars. "I'd like to think you'd come to me if things are that impossible," he continued eventually in his ancient voice. "But, Thad, I have to warn you. Sometimes there are no bolt-holes."

He fiddled with his cigar paraphernalia again and then said, "Life is a funny thing. Sometimes there seem to be no rules at all. Like young Chloe. She flits back and forth between centuries. Now, you've done the same, so I'm waiting to find out what's going to happen next. I keep thinking there have to be reasons for everything, especially for you being here. You've livened up my world, young Thad, and I'm grateful."

As though he were embarrassed, he turned and said good-bye and then walked to the cannon. I knew this was his way of ending the conversation but, once again, I felt frustrated. Mr. White had more ways of ending things when he didn't want to talk than anyone else I knew. He'd already slithered his way out of answering hard questions too many times to remember.

Breakfast brought even more frustration. Mr. Murray had news. He'd been called back to Los Angeles by his studio. "I'm flying out this afternoon."

"Dad!" Chloe looked like she might cry. "I was just getting used to having you around all the time."

Mr. Murray pulled her close and hugged her. "You're only missing two days, Scrap. Then you're off to school yourself. Now, will you do me a favor and pack for yourself and Thad? I need to talk to him."

Mr. Murray led me to a seat overlooking Lady's Cove. His face looked serious, and I wondered what I'd done. What he told me absolutely astounded me. I was, according to him, the richest boy in Australia. Part of me laughed. I was a convict kid who had stolen to feed my brothers and sisters. But when Mr. Murray went on to explain, I sort of understood.

When Chloe had pulled me through the brick with her, Lord and Lady Peter didn't know when, or if, I'd be back. So

Lord Peter kept me on Wahmurra's payroll. Billy had as well. The savings accumulated at something called compound interest and, as no money was ever withdrawn, it eventually became enormous. It was rolled into a trust fund that funded all kinds of things from the interest. He told me some of them, but my mind was useless. I just couldn't get over the fact that I had spending money.

Mr. White looked after the Compton Trust, and he'd made some incredibly smart investments. Mr. Murray said people called him Midas White, because everything he touched made money. Both he and Mr. Murray were my guardians. I didn't mind that. I was used to people telling me what I could or couldn't do. But the money thing was different. I had no idea what I thought about that.

In any case, I wouldn't have time to think. Just as Mr. Murray finished, the helicopter arrived and, when we walked over to the pad, Chloe and Tyce were waiting. The morning had one more huge shock. I was going to Sydney in it.

In 1833, I'd never imagined flying through the air. It seemed impossible. Now I started to worry. What would happen if the helicopter fell? Would I smash and die? Would it send me back to 1833?

As soon as the door opened, Chloe climbed into it. Mr. Murray sort of pushed me up the stairs and showed me how to buckle myself up. I looked across to Chloe, "Aren't you scared?"

"I've been flying ever since I can remember," she told me with a shrug. Then she seemed to understand I was not quite as blasé about it as she was, so she squeezed my hand. "It will be all right, Thad. I promise. Truly."

The helicopter lifted off almost immediately, and I gripped my seat like I was fighting off death. Too much was happening. I wasn't sure if it was because I was leaving

Wahmurra again, or the genuine love I'd felt from Mr. White. In any case, the helicopter's noise was the very worst thing I'd heard, and I clamped the sound mufflers tightly against my ears.

But soon I got interested and tried to work out where everything was. The Karuah River looked like a creek. At one point houses were everywhere I looked. Australia had always been dry. We'd battled drought twice at Wahmurra. I wondered if some magic had provided water for all these thousands and thousands of people. When we reached Sydney, the Opera House's sails sparkled white in the sun, and I leaned against Chloe, pulled her earphones off and pointed to the sail-roof. "Is there anything, anywhere, that's more magical and beautiful?"

Very quickly, though, I got a different definition of magical when we flew into Sydney Airport. I hadn't realized just how gigantic some planes were, and they looked like huge babies tethered to their mothers. Then we landed, and it was time for good-bye hugs and last minute warnings.

I was out on the water early the next morning. There were no watchers in the trees. Just water so calm that it was hard to remember a wind could suddenly whip it into a frenzied fury smashing against docks and shore. Chloe and I pooled our money the next day and, with the help of Mr. Murray's credit card, took Tyce to Chloe's favorite restaurant, Doyle's. As Chloe ate her Lobster Mornay and I bit into my Balmain Bugs, I wanted this meal to last forever. It was kind of like a last supper.

5

The next morning though, I couldn't wait to get rid of Chloe. She had obviously watched her father boss me around. Now she replicated him, walking into my bedroom with a handful of ties, and made me put each of them on until she thought the way I knotted them was "passable." Then she made me practice texting. I sent text after text until I texted, "Sod off."

After lunch, she put on her school uniform and transformed into a different person. Her school, Enderby, advertised itself as being a school for "young ladies," and I'd always wondered how Chloe fit in. Now, I had my answer. Gran had been right all along, and clothes did make a person. But when we walked out to the car, Chloe jammed her school hat on and tried to make a sexy pout. I laughed. Gran wasn't right, because my so unladylike Chloe was back.

"It's ridiculous to have to wear this. It's not like we're going by public transport, but it's the rule," she grumbled after Tyce started driving. "When we're between our homes and school, we're in public, and in public we wear uniform."

I snickered, both at the thought of getting dressed up for an hour's ride in Gran's car and also because Chloe was suddenly so concerned with rules. She caught my snicker and smirked. "Don't laugh now, Thad. You'll see. King William's has the exact same rule. I can't wait to see you in your boater."

I had no idea what she meant. "Boater?"

"It's a straw hat that was popular ages ago. Men wore them when they were on boats. Maybe Methuselah did as well, because they've been around forever and, for some reason, a bunch of Sydney schools have made them part of their uniforms. Like I said, you'll see."

Tyce pulled the car over. "Mr. White said you two squabble like five year olds. No more or I quit."

We shut up. I'd expected the drive to take forever, but it was over in a blink and we were at Enderby. The school was huge. I'd never expected one could be so big. It had all kinds of things I'd never thought of a school having. Like an aquatic center and a theatre.

"It's like a small college back home," Tyce commented.

"Wait till you see King William's. It's almost twice as big. Now, come along. I want to show you my pride and joy."

She surprised both Tyce and me when she took us to a chapel. It really was extraordinary. Not quite in the Opera House's league, but almost. From a distance it looked like a sculpture of huge hands in prayer. Inside, my mouth kind of dropped when what I'd thought was clever architecture turned out to be the organ's pipes.

Tyce didn't like it. "Modern and churches don't mix for me," he shrugged semi-apologetically.

Chloe looked hurt. "Why? It makes our singing sound beautiful. Plus, I feel good in here."

"A building can't make you feel good. Why when I was…" I stopped when she pinched me, and I remembered that Tyce didn't know about my convict days. I went back to my original thought. "It's silly to think buildings can make you holy or something. Only God can do that."

"Didn't say holy. I said good. Silly or not, that's what

happens," Chloe said and shrugged.

I mimicked her shrug. "So now we've replaced God with buildings? But if that's so, you should have a huge list of them for the times you...?"

"Stop it, you two. Now Chloe, what's next?"

"Dakin House."

Dakin was where Chloe lived at Enderby. I'd actually been there when we crashed into her century, but I didn't remember much. As soon as we came into view, Chloe's friends rushed over, hugged her and screamed in impossibly high voices. It made me sad. She must have sensed that, because she pulled away from her friends, ran back to us and kissed my cheek. I blushed and, while she shook hands with Tyce, I touched my cheek. Tyce tried to make conversation on our back to Gran's, but I just stared out the window.

The Thad and Chloe days were over.

The next morning Dr. Mansfield greeted me like I was a prized patient and personally took me to the surgery center at Greenway. When I'd climbed onto a bed and been settled with blood pressure things on my finger and stuff, he and a couple of other doctors told me what to expect during and after the operation.

They had a picture of my leg, and I saw why I'd so much trouble walking. One of them explained where they were going to break it again, showed me how they'd "pin" it back together. After the operation, I'd see a tube draining fluid from my leg, a needle taped to the back of my hand where water and pain killers dripped into my body, and enough plaster on my leg to keep my bones absolutely still while they mended. "And," one of them said in a kind of farewell, "you'll feel groggy and thirsty. That's normal, though."

I had no idea what his definition of normal was when I

became conscious again. I wondered if I was in hell. I was thirsty, like I'd been warned. But the pain? I somehow hadn't expected to feel such excruciating pain again and particularly not in this magical century of Chloe's. I couldn't stop groaning, and a nurse hurried over and pushed a button. She told me I'd feel better, but I knew she was keeping something back. Sure enough, Dr. Mansfield came into the room seconds later.

"What's the matter?" I croaked.

"We have a problem."

No. They hadn't fixed my leg. Would I even walk again?

Dr. Mansfield tried to smile, but his eyes looked worried. "Frank Bundy's somehow found out there's someone connected with Mr. White in here. He's been stalking the room we'd planned to put you in."

Frank Bundy seemed so long ago and, given my level of pain, I found it hard to care. "What does this mean? Are you sure it's him?"

"No one else has his hair color."

Ol' Bundy has.

"So?"

One syllable, and my voice climbed an octave. The thought of Ol' Bundy prowling around obviously affected me. I flushed, but Dr. Mansfield didn't seem to notice. He just went on explaining his plan.

"Well if you don't object, we'll hide you in plain sight in the general wards. We'll keep a security man outside the room you would have had and hope that it fools Bundy. But your room won't be what you're used to."

I looked at him and grinned. He was one of the few people who knew everything about me. "Used to? Now or then? Sir, I don't care. I know Tyce is supposed to give me lessons while I'm here, so anything that keeps me out of Frank Bundy's tabloid is good news to me."

"Mr. White said he's sorry. He won't be able to visit you. Not with Bundy snooping around."

Once I agreed to the plan and settled into a room, I could see what Dr. Mansfield meant. Compared with my previous suite in Greenway, it was plain and kind of depressing. I wished I could have gone back to Wahmurra, but Dr. Mansfield said he wouldn't let me out of his sight until all the pins and things had been removed.

The days that followed were almost unendurable. If I'd been able to walk, I think I would have snuck out at night and begged rides until I reached Wahmurra. Even Tyce became boring. "All you talk about is vowel sounds, sound centers, and rhythms," I told him.

He handed me a voice recorder. "That's what I'm getting paid for. Now, read this again."

"I don't want a mid-anything accent. What's the matter with the way I talk anyway?"

He stood up and pushed my wheelchair outside. It felt good to have the sun on me, and he'd forgotten about sunscreens. He let me soak up the sun for a few minutes and then said, "I've got a joke. Old, but good."

I perked up. "Bring it on."

He smiled. "Just after Christmas a Mr. and Mrs. Jones flew here from California. They wanted to see the New Year's fireworks go off on the Harbour Bridge."

I understood. The New Year fireworks were spectacular. We'd gone out on Mr. Murray's boat and watched them, and I could see why people might come from America for them. "And?"

"After they landed and checked into a hotel, they went for a walk. But Mrs. Jones forgot that cars drive on the opposite side of the road here. She stepped right in front of a bus. They rushed her to hospital, and Mr. Jones followed in a taxi."

I nodded, encouraging him to continue. "So," Tyce went on, "when he arrived here, he had to go through admissions to get the paper work done. Eventually he took the elevator and started walking down the hallway to Mrs. Jones's room when he heard one of the cleaning staff say, 'Don't worry about C121. She only came in to die.'"

"That's not funny."

"No, it isn't, but that's the joke. The cleaning person really said, 'She only came in today.' But, because she said it at the front of her mouth, it made a nasal sound and came out as 'to die.' Thad, that's the way you sound, and that's why I've been trying to get you to center your words. Get it?"

I got it, and the silly joke helped me understand what he'd been trying to do. I began working hard and, almost as a reward, the drain came out of my leg and I met my therapist, Meris Hatcher. "She's just like you," I told Tyce. "A slave driver."

Now that I had a little more mobility, Wahmurra became more of a temptation. When he saw my fidgets, Dr. Mansfield ordered me to settle down. "You're just upsetting yourself. The more you fret, the longer it's going to take. We need to get everything stable before you can go."

I gave up. The only piece of good news was a couple of reports of Frank Bundy still trying to get through the hospital's security. One morning I tried to work on Billy's number puzzle, but it only made me more frustrated and Meris Hatcher took it away.

The next morning I woke up, and Mr. Murray smiled at me. "Good morning."

"I want out. I want out so badly, Mr. Murray."

"And I'm here to spring you out. At least, out of here."

Just simple words, but what a difference. Birds sang, the sky was blue, everything was suddenly right in my world. "Wahmurra?"

"Nope. We tried. Mr. White and me. But Dr. Mansfield wants you where he can see you and under medical supervision. So Mr. White talked him into something else, and we're going to move you by ambulance later today."

6

This was what Chloe called good news, bad news. I'd heard the good, I was leaving Greenway. Now as I waited for the bad, I felt incredibly happy. Mr. White had understood. He hadn't risked coming to Greenway, but I was beginning to understand that this ancient man really cared about me. Maybe even loved me. If he'd had an idea, I was all for it. Then I had a truly wonderful thought.

"Am I going back to Los Angeles with you?"

Mr. Murray laughed. "Not even Mr. White could make that happen. No, it's much more ordinary. Dr. Mansfield wants you where he's only a phone call away and where you'll be under constant supervision. So Mr. White's booked you into King William's. Not the school part. The infirmary. It's like a little hospital, but nurses will monitor you the same way as here and report back to Dr. Mansfield. What do you think?"

I slumped back on the bed. "It will still be a prison."

Mr. Murray looked frustrated, but his voice was gentle when he said, "Thad, stop whining. Yes, King William's *will* be a prison if you keep thinking that way. But, it can also be fun and an adventure. That's what you've got to work out. As long as you keep moaning and grumbling and wishing you could go back to the past, you're going to be both miserable and miserable to be around. Face facts. You're no longer Thaddeus Compton, convict number 30/529 with a bum leg. It's been fixed, and there's no going back on that. You speak differently, so think differently."

I turned my face to the wall, as unwilling to face him as I was to face facts.

But Mr. Murray waited till I turned back and looked him in the face. "Thad, I know it's hard. But, you talk all the time about God. Seems to me he's given you a second chance in life. I don't know how that's going to work out and neither do you. But, truly, are you arrogant enough to throw away one of his blessings?"

He stopped talking for a moment, and I could see that he was frustrated. He walked up and down in short steps until he worked out what he wanted to berate me with next. But his voice was softer when he started again, "Thad, remember what you wanted more than everything else in the world? Don't you remember when you were a convict you told Chloe that you wanted to go to a proper school? Well, it seems that God has given you your wish. You've got the chance to go to one of the best schools in the world, and you're sulking? Grow up, Thad."

I hadn't thought about it that way and, when I did, I had no answers. "Sorry. I am grateful. I'll go anywhere." I allowed the idea to trickle through my mind and then I sat up. "I'll be close to Chloe's school, won't I?"

"Ten, fifteen minutes away. A mere taxi ride. She'll be able to come for visits."

I began smiling. "And you, sir? Will you be here, or are you going back to Los Angeles? And Tyce? Will he transfer also?"

"I'll be here for the next few months, and Tyce will stay at a small hotel near the school. He's almost at the point of signing off on your accent, so he'll just teach you ordinary stuff now so you don't make a perfect fool of yourself."

The transfer to King William's infirmary took place that night with a paranoid Dr. Mansfield following the ambulance. He fidgeted while the nurses settled me into my new bed, checking and rechecking everything. Then, he stood at the bottom of the bed and made a steeple with his fingers.

"Don't think for a moment, this is good-bye," he said eventually. "Never had a more interesting case. Would have done it for free, but don't tell Mr. White that."

I hid a grin. I knew Mr. White had almost god-like status with him. I had been Dr. Mansfield's patient for years. Truly. Mr. White paid him a retainer and how he'd known I'd need Dr. Mansfield, much less make him my personal doctor years before I arrived in the twenty-first century, was one of those questions Mr. White found ways of avoiding.

I was about to ask Dr. Mansfield if he knew anything when he spoilt my day by saying, "Roll up your sleeve, young Thad. I've got one last set of shots for you."

I glared. "Mr. White promised there wouldn't be any more after the operation."

"Well, yes. We both thought that. But we both forgot that you hadn't been immunized against measles, chicken pox etc. They're given automatically nowadays, and we just plain forgot about you needing them."

I have to say this about Dr. Mansfield. He was a great doctor, and I barely felt the shots. I pretended to, of course. Moaning and groaning like a regular diva, but he knew and understood. I was kind of sad when he packed everything away and looked at me, "Take care, Thad. Do your rehab and remember, I'll be keeping an eye on you."

I hid a grin as he walked away. The old beggar liked me! I supposed I'd miss him. He was part of the core group that knew everything about me. For a brief moment, I felt despair. Once again, I was on my own and would have to survive in an alien place, but then my phone played its Rocky tune. Chloe had somehow broken her school's rules and texted, "C u in 5 days."

After breakfast, the next morning, I Googled King William's and found maps of the school. It took a while to figure out which side of the infirmary I was in, but soon I began sorting out which buildings I could see from the window.

The next few days were fun. The school day started almost as early as my convict days had. Soon after dawn, some students ran across to what I thought was a food building, and half an hour later climbed into waiting buses. A few boys, day ones I assumed because of their boaters, joined them.

About an hour later boys in army uniforms drilled outside on one of the cricket grounds, others filtered towards the swimming pool, and still more filtered towards the food building. The stream of day boys arriving became a flood, and the buses returned and disgorged boys in maroon and green athletic gear. Then a bell rang, everyone raced to the classrooms and King William's was silent.

During class time I worked out with the school's physiotherapist. I thought he was the drill sergeant also because he never talked properly. He just roared. "You're not fit enough," was his constant rant.

Well, he might have been a drill sergeant, but he wasn't Ol' Bundy. He didn't terrify me, so I snapped back, "What makes you think I should be? I've been in hospitals for the last three months."

That shut him up. For a while. He scaled his aggression down and I finally felt I made progress. I wasn't as strong as I used to be, but I began to think that the ground between my pessimistic expectations and those of Dr. Mansfield might be reachable.

Tyce did his best to teach me about the modern world. I watched video after video. At first I looked forward to them, then they bored me. Once you figured their story out, they were basically the same, and I hated the way their music tried to manipulate my emotions. When Tyce left to go into Sydney, I pulled out Billy's puzzle. It was the first real uninterrupted time I'd had to think about it.

I decided to do a lot of guessing and started writing B I L L Y above the letters of the last word, and decode 7, 12, 19 as T H E. After playing around with those letters, I guessed the last two words of the message were Double Bay, and then my sheet looked like this:

I | 99, 70, 1 | 188, 92, 26 | **L**, 33, 107, 93 | 10, **I**, 43, **H**, 93. | **YOU** | 1, 61, 272, 20 | 131 | 272, 20, 22 | 100, 10, 55 | 43, 272, **E**, 20, 54 | 4, **T**, 272, **I**, 257, 256, **D** | 118, 15, **H**, 63, 67, **L** | **J**, 131, 15, 23, 95, 80. | 188, 86, **U** | 223, 21, 21, 23, 20, 22 | 29, 6, 31, 62, 213.

93, 112, 71, **D** | 93, 112, 95, 272, 256 | 105, 4 | 97, 92, 272, 95 | 93, 112, 255, 50 | 21, 54, 95 | 1, 6, 188 | **B**, 95, 93, 27, 256, 20, 54 | 67, 26, 272 | 17, 72, 272, 223, **D**, 84. | **L**, 21, 42, 23 | **B**, 32, 29, 9, 50, 22 | **THE** | 18, 103, 102, 111, 112 | 99, 96, 86, 54, 256 | 102, 272, 21, 97 | **THE** | 115, L, 86, 82, 272 | 9, 50 | **THE** | 5, 92, 92, 93 | 112, 92, 116, 4, 19 | 110, 54 | **DOUBLE** | **BAY**.

BILLY

I had a ridiculous sense of achievement. The numbers meant something, and I thought Billy might be telling me where he'd left something for me in Gran's house. I looked at the puzzle again and decided that 110, 54 might mean IN and that 188, 86 U might be YOU.

Mr. Murray had been so right. Many numbers could represent one letter, like the ones that were "ls" in Billy. So unless I could figure out what book or document Billy had used, I was at a dead end.

I thought back to the first clue. Billy had told me to think hard about Leonardo da Vinci. He hadn't said research, so that meant I should be able to figure out the clue. But every time I thought I kept getting entangled with the three beers. When Mrs. Cox, my nurse, wheeled my lunch in, I felt relief.

"What do you know about Leonardo da Vinci?"

"Other than the Mona Lisa?" When I nodded, she went on slowly, "Well he lived sometime in the Renaissance and he's supposed to have invented all kind of machines."

I took the cover off my salad. She knew the same things as everyone else. She started for the door, and then turned back. "There's the mirror writing, of course. He wrote diaries in it, I think."

"Mirror writing?"

"It's writing backwards. You need a mirror to read it properly." She grabbed her pen and a bit of paper and concentrated as she wrote my name backwards "It's not right, but it should give you an idea."

I looked at the paper and, just like that, I knew what Billy meant.

When Mrs. Cox came back, she looked at me and grinned. "I don't know what was in that lunch, but it sure made you a happy boy."

"I am. Happy, that is. But Mrs. Cox? Would it be possible to see a chaplain?"

"Chaplain Thomas? He's not on your approved visitors' list."

"Mr. Murray would allow it," I said. When she still looked doubtful, I pulled out my heavy hitter. "So would Mr. White. Why not call him?"

Her head jerked up at the suggestion that she call Mr. White. I'd seen other people react in the same way and I still didn't understand. Didn't they see the gentle, fragile man I knew? On the other hand, Mr. White had his finger in so many financial pies, according to Mr. Murray, that he might control their wages or mortgages.

"I'll phone the headmaster," she said when she recovered. Fifteen minutes later she came back with the news that Chaplain Thomas would come in an hour's time.

"Thank you. And, please Mrs. Cox, could you ask him to bring a *Book of Common Prayer* with him please?"

"A what?"

I felt like bashing my head on my wheelchair. Mr. Murray had told me people were post-Christian, whatever that meant. Chloe had warned me to think before I spoke. But I hadn't. Thought, that is. And, as I looked at the genuine amazement on Mrs. Cox's face, I realized I hadn't listened to them either. I'd expected that the prayer book, something even the most ignorant convict on Wahmurra would have known about, would have been general knowledge. Suddenly my grasp on the twenty-first century felt a lot more tentative.

I explained what I wanted, and she stared at me as though I were an exotic animal in the Taroonga Park Zoo. "You want a prayer book to read?" she said, and her voice seemed a little higher than usual. "You really are a strange one."

She walked off, and I knew the prayer book had made it to the very top of her list of strange requests by Dubbees.

Chaplain Thomas was older than I expected and had a sense of world-weariness. He held himself like a soldier, but his eyes were kind, and his smile charmed. "Mrs. Cox told me to bring a prayer book," he said after shaking hands. Then he handed it over.

I started to flip through it, then stopped. I didn't

recognize anything.

"What's the matter?" he asked.

"I wanted the *Book of Common Prayer*."

"You've got it. I brought the very latest version."

There was crankiness in my voice when I mini-exploded, "Nobody's modernized Shakespeare have they? Why muck around with the prayer book?"

He looked at me in much the same way as Mrs. Cox had. Then he seemed to see something, because his voice was gentle when he asked, "Why is the old one so important, Thad?"

Because Billy used it for a code. I bit the answer off in my throat. Even if I'd said it, I knew that wasn't the reason I was so upset. The prayer book was the straw that broke the camel's back. It was something that shouldn't have changed. But it had, and I was fed up with changes. Not even my hair was off limits. When Tyce had taken me for a haircut, the man had asked if I wanted the front part colored.

At some point I realized Chaplain Thomas had begun talking. "If you need the old one so desperately, look it up on the internet. I guarantee that it's there."

Of course. What an idiot I'd been. I'd even told Chloe that the internet was her century's equivalent of a junk yard because it had everything. Now Mrs. Cox and Chaplain Thomas thought I was a raving lunatic when all I'd had to do was make a Google search.

So caught up in feeling stupid, I almost missed the start of Chaplain Thomas's sentence, "There's more going on here than a prayer book. Thad, I know you're Mr. White's long-lost grandson or something. But I also know something's troubling you deep inside. Do you want to tell me about it?"

And get shut up like the kangaroos in a zoo?

7

I bit my lips to keep them shut. How could this man understand when Chloe couldn't? I almost wet myself when I heard myself blurt out, "I've been in hospitals for three months now."

Chaplain Thomas looked puzzled, but he settled himself a little more comfortably in his chair. "And?" he said in his gentle voice.

"Sir. I've only been to church twice in that time. I feel awful. Like I'm deserting God or something, and I think he needs all his friends to stand by him right now."

The chaplain's lips twitched, and his eyebrows climbed high on his forehead. The lazy I-can-wait-forever attitude disappeared. "Is it the habit of going to church you miss, or is it God, Thad?"

I looked at the floor, at the shiny rims of my wheelchair, anywhere but at Chaplain Thomas while I thought. "It's not God," I said finally. "I know he's with me here, and everywhere. But I feel like I'm the only person who knows him and I can't understand that."

"Well, now you know you're not alone. I believe in him."

"Is it only because you're paid to?" A second after I'd said the words, I realized how rude they were. "Sorry. I meant, if you weren't a chaplain would it be different?"

The silence stretched while, I think, both of us tried to work each other out. He blinked first. He shifted in his armchair and looked me straight in the eye. "Thad, I know you've been held a prisoner. I don't know the details. I don't need to. But, I've been one as well, and I do know how corrosive it is to bottle stuff up because you don't know whom to trust. Forty years ago I spent months in a bamboo cage."

He had my complete attention. A bamboo cage? A chain-gang sounded so much better.

"The enemy was the Viet Cong and they poked me with sharpened sticks to try to get me to talk about my unit. I was isolated, so I didn't know where I was or even if there were other cages. I knew I was by myself, that no one could help me." He looked away for such a long time that I'd thought he'd gone back somehow to his bamboo cage. I imagined him crouching, twisting and turning to escape those bamboo sticks. Then he turned back to me with his gentle smile and said, "No one, that is, except God."

I felt part of me melt and, while I couldn't tell him everything, I knew he'd understand stuff that Mr. Murray and Chloe didn't. "How did you survive?"

"Two ways. First and foremost, the war ended after a couple of weeks. Before that, though, I had a secret weapon. I'd been studying up on becoming a chaplain. When the beatings began, I went deep into my mind and recited bits of services that I'd memorized."

"Like the burial one?" I said, intending it as a joke.

He didn't get it. Instead he said, "Exactly. Guys died all the time, and we couldn't stop to bury them. So I memorized the service, said it as fast as I could over the bodies and then raced to catch up with my unit. That service kept me sane." He looked across at me. "That war's in the history books, so I don't expect you to understand."

I leaned forward. "But, sir, I do. Understand, that is. I was flogged once. I knew what was going to happen, because I'd had to watch other floggings. I knew the whip would rip my back into shreds."

Even now, I could only talk about that horrible time in a whisper. Dubbees jogged by outside, and I sensed I straddled two different worlds. They would never understand how knowing what was going to happen made facing my flogging so much harder.,

But God had sent a friend. Chaplain Thomas did understand, and my voice was louder when I continued, "Waiting for it to happen was the hardest part. It wasn't the pain so much, it was how I'd react to it. I was terrified of disgracing myself by screaming, or something. A friend told me to recite bits of the Bible over and over, so that's what I did. And when I couldn't remember any more, I did Latin declensions as well. Oh, and I prayed. Prayed like I was on my death bed."

For an instant Chaplain Thomas looked amazed. Floggings, Latin declensions and fourteen year old Dubbees didn't fit together. "Obviously the Lord answered. Thad, I can't help with the past, but I can with the present. Why don't we have a short service now, just you and me? Would you like that?"

Was he serious? One-on-one church sounded weird, and I could imagine Mrs. Cox's face if she walked in on us. But, at Wahmurra, priests used to come occasionally to hear confession for the few men who were Catholic. It would be the same, sort of.

"Yes."

Chaplain surprised me again when we finished. "I'll arrange for Nurse Cox to wheel you across to chapel each morning. We'll have Morning Prayer together. Just you and me. Nurse too, if she wants to join in."

An insane burst of glee burbled up inside me at the thought of Mrs. Cox participating in Morning Prayer. I'd have to explain it to her, of course. "Thank you."

After he stood up, Chaplain Thomas looked back for a long moment. "Thad? A last question. Why is this so important to you?"

I almost told him that what he saw wasn't the real Thad Compton. That I was only a twenty-first century upgrade. I looked better and was certainly better looked after than I'd ever been. Thanks to Tyce no one raised an eyebrow about my new accent.

But in my heart, in the secret places of my being, I mourned. I still grieved for my old Cockney way of "torking." Sometimes I couldn't remember my family's faces. I knew they were dead, and no matter what I did that I'd never see them again. That faint hope was gone. And I grieved for convict-age Wahmurra and my friends among its tough convicts. I almost laughed when I thought of what they'd say about this new pretty-boy Thad.

I really missed my old, slow world and its silences. I mourned sitting on the dock after work and just looking at the water and dreaming impossible dreams. Even Chloe had understood how perfect that was when she'd been back in 1833. Now she was always texting someone, usually me. That wasn't silence.

I couldn't tell Chaplain Thomas this, no matter how sympathetic he seemed. Instead I told him my most secret fear. "I don't want to lose God. He knows who I am. He's answered my prayers, even secret ones that I never told anyone. Sir, God's the only thing I can count on who won't change, and I don't want to be a fair weather friend and only talk to him when I'm in trouble."

8

After Chaplain Thomas left, I gave in to the inevitable and texted Chloe, telling her that I knew how to decode Billy's message. Then I maneuvered my wheelchair along the hallway to Matron's office.

"May I have lots of paper and some pencils, please?"

"And where do you plan to use my paper and pencils, young Thad?"

I looked around. By the time I finished, Matron had produced an adjustable table and set it up in a sunlit alcove. "Chaplain's visit has done you a world of good." Then she looked me over and smiled. "Funny that we're surprised when he does good, because that's a chaplain's job, isn't it? Doing good, I mean."

I grinned and, after she'd gone, I picked up one sheet of paper, folded it in half lengthwise, and wrote the letters A-M down one side and N-Z down the other. Then, on a new sheet, I began writing numbers in columns. I'd just reached 272 when I heard hurried footsteps. The door burst open and Chloe stood in front of me in her green Enderby dress and the detested white panama hat with its green and gold hatband on her head.

"I just texted you. What are you doing here? How

did…"

Chloe cut me off. "Parent-teacher interviews. It's a half-day, so Dad had a taxi bring me here. He'll pick me up at five." She looked at the papers and frowned. "What's with the columns?"

"I figured out Billy's code. It's CREED 3. It doesn't have anything to do with beer."

She frowned as though she thought I must be crazy. "What do you mean? Creed 3? You said it would be common knowledge. I've never heard of it."

"It's the St. Athanasius creed." I laughed when Chloe glared at me. She looked just like Mrs. Cox. The angst I'd had with Chaplain Thomas had disappeared. "Chloe, that's why Billy told me to think hard. There's the Apostle's creed, of course…"

"Thad, there's no *of course*. Nobody knows creeds anymore. Nobody. Outside of church, that is."

What did her world believe in? Every civilization I'd read about had creeds, although they called them different words, like *taboos*. "Well, if you think of the Apostle's creed as creed 1. It's the first one. Written when people could still remember who the apostles were, I think."

"You mean the ones in the Bible?" Chloe interjected.

I ignored her. "The next one's the Nicaea creed, so, call it creed number 2. So, creed 3 has to be the St. Athanasius one. I hated it when I was a convict, because it's long and we had to stand without shuffling our feet until the chaplain finished. I grumbled every time, and Billy must have remembered."

"I've never heard of it, and I go to an Anglican school," Chloe frowned.

"That's why it's so brilliant. Billy picked something that was in plain sight, something that I'd know about if I thought hard, but was totally obscure to most people. Your dad said it might be a long document and, believe me, that's exactly what the Athanasian creed is. Long."

"Okay," Chloe said after she'd thought about it forever. "It's better than anything else we've thought of."

"It's the only thing we've thought of. So, what do you want to do? Read or write?"

"Write."

I started reading out the first letter of each word in the creed, and Chloe dutifully wrote it beside a number. "It's funny," she said after a few minutes. "So far the most common letters are T and W. I only have one D, and no J or R, much less a Q, X or Z."

We stopped at the first R, number 272, because it was the highest number Billy used. Then it was a simple matter of reading numbers out, and Chloe translating them into letters. "We've got it," she announced, when the final word spelled Billy. "But, it's weird. He's talking to you, that's for sure:

I SAW YOU LAST NIGHT. YOU WORE A RED AND GREEN STRIPED SCHOOL JACKET. THAD, THERE IS MORE THAN ONE WAY BETWEEN OUR WORLDS.

LOOK BEHIND THE FIFTH STONE FROM THE GARDEN DOOR IN THE FIFTH ROW FROM THE FLOOR IN THE BOAT HOUSE IN DOUBLE BAY.

BILLY

I couldn't speak, but Chloe jumped up, sending papers and pencils in all directions. "He must have left something there. A present. Oh, I can't wait till the weekend when I can go home."

This weekend and I'm still stuck here? "Chloe, you cannot look for Billy's present without me. That's unfair. I absolutely forbid it."

"I won't, don't worry. Promise, but haven't you heard? Your cast's coming off on Thursday. Dr. Mansfield thinks you won't even need a walking boot—just crutches."

It had been so long that I'd almost given up on the thought of walking normally—well, half-way normally. I thought about it and almost missed the rest of what she was saying, "Dad's picking you up just before two on Friday and officially enrolling you as a Dubbee. That is, providing you don't do something totally stupid and have to go back to Greenway. Anyway, after that, you collect me at Enderby, and we go home to the boat house. Thad, this is so exciting. I can't wait."

She jumped up and did a little dance. I looked at her, saw all the happiness and joy in her face, and wondered what I'd done to deserve such a friend.

There was always a price for everything. That was one thing I'd learned. How high would this particular price be? Would gratitude be enough?

Friday couldn't come fast enough. After lunch, I pressed my nose against my window like a kid gawking at some treasure in a shop window. My leg felt funny without the cast, and I flexed my muscles to try and sort the kinks out.

I felt excited and jittery. Like I couldn't wait for Mr. Murray to come, but at the same time, I was petrified. I hadn't had this same mix of emotions since I'd sat below decks on the convict ship. It had just anchored in Sydney Cove, so I wanted to walk on land again, but the thought of the unknown country in which I'd be a prisoner terrified me.

Now, I felt the exact same way—keyed up, energized, but so very apprehensive.

And, after the weekend, I'd be completely on my own.

Dr. Mansfield had signed me out of the infirmary himself after poking and prodding me to his heart's content.

Tyce had flown off to a gig in Europe, Mr. Murray would stay in Gran's house, and Chloe would return to Enderby.

But that was okay. I'd survived the convict world of 1833 and two stints in a twenty-first century hospital. Surely I could manage the privileged world of King William's School for Boys. Best of all, Ol' Bundy, if he were around, would never find me amongst the hundreds of Dubbees in the same uniform.

I was still stuck in thought when Mr. White's Rolls Royce stopped in front of the infirmary. It took Mrs. Cox's gasp to bring me back to my senses.

"I'd heard about that car. Never thought I'd see it."

"Why? It's kind of old. Why is it so special?"

She went off in a long paean of praise. Mr. White's Rolls was almost a hundred years old. Several royals had been chauffeured around in it. Blah, blah, and so on. I really couldn't figure out what most of it meant but, after she settled me into the wheelchair, she resumed her role of medical grump.

"Remember to use your crutches, Thad. Your leg is still very weak. I don't usually say this, but we'll miss you. Matron said just last night that you've been a model patient."

I felt sorry for all the bad things I'd thought about her when I said good-bye but, outside, the air felt so wonderful that I forgot to be grumpy. Just the wind ruffling my hair was enough to make me smile at the entire world.

Mr. White's Rolls still felt like a comfy armchair. I still hadn't made my mind up about twenty-first century transportation. Nothing yet had replaced the exhilaration of being in perfect harmony with a horse, or zipping out to the middle of the bay at Port Stephens in a rowboat. The Rolls was like being on a magic carpet. No excitement. No work required.

The school's administrative offices were only a short distance from the infirmary as the proverbial crow flew, but the road between them went by the main cricket oval. Its greenness took my breath away, and I wondered how much money it took to keep it so manicured-looking.

I returned to reality very quickly. When I tried to get out of the car, I fell. Mr. Murray helped me up and said rather crossly, "You'll have to practice, Thad. I won't be able to help when you come back here."

I shrugged. I knew what the problem was. I'd practiced on smooth infirmary floors, and the pebbly driveway had thrown me off-balance. Still I felt chastened as I followed Mr. Murray up the stairs and down a long hallway. When the headmaster's door opened, the first person I saw was Mr. White, and I realized that I'd learned one thing since coming into Chloe's world.

Whatever was wrong, I trusted Mr. White to fix it.

He put his hand on my shoulder again, and I appreciated one more thing. Mr. White rarely showed affection but, maybe, Chloe was right and he did really care about me. When he turned to the headmaster, I heard pride in his voice when he said, "Dr. Rivers, you know Zach of course, but this is Thaddeus Compton. Thad, this is Dr. Rivers, your headmaster."

Dr. Rivers looked absurdly young to hold such an important position. His blond hair was longer than the school allowed us Dubbees, and a smile lit his face. I'd seen people like him before. They usually charmed their way out of trouble. But Mr. White seemed to trust him, so I decided I'd wait before rushing to judgment.

Dr. Rivers shook Mr. Murray's hand first. "Zach, welcome back from Los Angeles." Then he turned to me and took my hand. "Thad, we're very pleased to have you finally here at King William's. We've been expecting you for a very long time."

A long time? If he was so eager to see me, why hadn't he come to the infirmary? I didn't know how to answer, so I just said, "Thank you."

Dr. Rivers took this reticence in stride. "Sit over here, young man. I want to run through the main rules of the school with and tell you your schedule for the next few weeks."

King William's main rules seemed to take five hours to "run through", and I couldn't imagine breaking any of them. I'd learned honesty and obedience the hard way. Then Dr. Rivers handed me two plastic oblongs. "This card is like a key. It opens the front door of your house and your room. This one," he said and held up the second oblong, "is your school identification card. You use it to borrow books from the library or charge things to your account at the school store. Treat them like gold and don't lose them. We charge a $75 replacement fee."

As I put both of them into my wallet, I saw that the identification card had my picture on it. I didn't know where and when it had been taken. Just more of Mr. White's magic.

I thought I was through, but Dr. Rivers hadn't finished. "Thad, you have an appointment in five minutes to be outfitted for your uniform. That should take you an hour. You're in School House, of course."

Of course? What was so special about School House? Why was it an "of course?"

Dr. River gave no answers when he went on, "Mr. Graham, your housemaster, will meet you in the shop and show you to your room and make sure you know your way around. Now, I know you have an *exeat*…"

When I looked bewildered, Dr. Rivers stopped. "Sorry. *Exeat* is a word for being away from school. Officially, that is. In your case, it means for this weekend, so the next time I'll see you will be back here for Chapel on Sunday night. Make sure you're in uniform."

I nodded, but he still had more to say. "We've decided to ease you into school slowly. We'll start you out in Year 9 and see how it goes. Afternoons only, at first. We'll have a better idea about where you are after Mr. Graham gives you a placement test on Monday. As Dr. Mansfield recommended exercise to strengthen your legs, I've arranged for you to go to our rowing center with the rowing team before school starts. When you come back, you'll work out with our physiotherapist, and then it's off to the classroom."

Once again I thought we were through, but Dr. Rivers scribbled something on a card. When he looked at me this time, I saw true concern and I revised my earlier opinion. I could probably trust him, so I listened carefully when he said, "Thad, if you have trouble, and any trouble at all, come here and talk to me. This is my private number. Keep it in your wallet and, please, don't flash it around. I don't want every Tom, Dick and Harry in the school phoning me. Like I said, it's for emergencies. Understand?"

I nodded again and carefully put the card into my wallet. "Thank you, sir."

I started to struggle to my feet, but Mr. Murray clamped a hand on my shoulder. "One minute, Thad. Dr. Rivers, a question if you don't mind. About Thad's placement test? What does Mr. Graham know about Thad?"

"Just a little more than the basic story Mr. White's been telling everyone. He knows that Thad was born in England and then mysteriously imprisoned. We've circulated rumors about that, making them all very vague. Some people think he was kidnapped in the Middle East. Others think something happened in Russia," Dr. Rivers answered with a surprisingly gleeful grin. "My personal favorite is the African pirates version."

The grin faded when he looked at me. "Thad, the school already understands that it owes a huge debt to the Thaddeus Compton Trust. I'll make a brief announcement in Monday's assembly that you're now part of our student body. Everybody will think you're a descendant of the Thaddeus they know about. Hopefully, the boys will have enough good manners not to ask personal questions."

"Ah," Mr. Murray said. "Thad, captured by pirates? I like it."

Dr. Rivers lost his smile. "Thad, you do understand that people will begin to connect you to the Compton Trust, don't you? That's why you were plain Thad Smith in the infirmary and why I didn't visit. I didn't want to hype your status."

He was talking gibberish now. I'd thought the Thad Smith thing was protection against Frank Bundy. But the Compton Trust? "Mr. Murray told me that some money had been invested in the school. I don't know much more than that."

Dr. Rivers looked across the room to Mr. White and gestured to him to continue the explanation.

"Thad, part of your money kept the school alive during the 1930's depression," Mr. White began in his whisper. "Didn't you notice the cricket oval?" After I nodded, he asked, "Did you see its name? It's the Thaddeus Compton Oval, named after you despite my objections. There's more than that, though. There are Compton scholarships and references to the Trust scattered everywhere. If you're asked about them, all you have to say is yes, you're connected to the Trust, but you don't know the ins and outs of it."

"That's true. I don't."

Mr. White's voice sounded very old when he

continued, "If someone becomes objectionable, tell them to ask Dr. Rivers or me about it."

Right, as though that would work. "But how can that oval be named after me? It's old, isn't it?"

"More than fifty, sixty years."

The headmaster's office wasn't the right place to follow up on this and my other questions, but I couldn't help myself. "If it's that old, there's no problem, is there? No one will think I'm the person it was named after. They'll think I'm a descendant, like Dr. Rivers said."

"Not if they find out the terms of the trust."

More gibberish and I felt grateful when Dr. Rivers took command of the interview again. "Now, Thad, just sign these papers and you can be on your way. Mr. White and I have more business to discuss. Off you go and get yourself kitted out. Don't forget. Next time I see you, I expect to see you in your suit and school tie. Until then, good bye."

9

I felt so relieved to have the interview over, I almost skipped my way to the store. Only my crutches stopped me. I'd have to do a lot of practicing at Gran's to be ready for Monday.

I felt happy. For the first time since I'd arrived, I had a road map. I knew about school stores from reading the Harry Potter books. I knew what the weekend at Gran's would be like, and I almost understood the rhythm of life at King William's.

Half an hour later I wondered how I could have compared myself to Harry Potter. I hadn't expected a wand to magically choose me. Neither had I imagined the mounds of clothes on the counter that the shop ladies called essentials. I had $81 left from the $100 Mr. Murray had given me as a Christmas present. From what I could see, it wouldn't pay for one quarter of one mound.

When Dr. Rivers had said I'd need an hour to be outfitted, I hadn't believed him. Now I wondered if we'd be done in a week's time. I held my arms out till they ached, had my waist measured by ladies with tape measures. Stopping them was impossible. They even measured the inside length of my legs.

The mounds were impressive. I had five pairs of grey shorts, five sage-striped white shirts, and six pairs of gray knee length socks. There were two green and maroon striped ties for everyday school, and a silk one for chapel, special occasions and off-campus.

Shivers went up my spine when I saw the maroon and green tie. It reminded me of the one Billy tied his letters with. How had Billy got it? How had he even known what King William's colors were?

While I thought, the ladies started more mounds and added black leather lace-up shoes with a polishing kit, two belts, two grey v-necked sweaters with maroon and green stripes around the neck band, and a green fleecy jacket. Then they brought out two maroon jackets and asked me to try them on for size. While they fiddled with sleeve lengths, I remembered Billy's note and turned to Mr. Murray. "Shouldn't I have a green and red striped one?"

"They're honors blazers," one of the ladies informed me in a voice that bordered on reverential. "You have to earn one. Maybe, in a few years, you'll be lucky. Now, Mr. Murray, does Thad have a navy suit, or should we add one? He'll need it for Sunday chapel and special occasions."

"He already has his suit. He'll wear it when he comes back on Sunday," Mr. Murray answered.

Just when I thought the number of clothes couldn't get bigger, the ladies brought out a straw boater hat and the green and maroon hatband that he'd seen on boys from the infirmary's windows. When they explained that it had to be worn off campus, I felt grateful that I was a boarder and wouldn't have to wear the stupid thing all the time.

"Count your blessings," a lady told him. "In my son's day, boaters had to be worn to school from everywhere, even the boarding houses."

"Why?"

They ignored me, and I eyed the mountains of clothes with trepidation. "This has to be awfully expensive," I whispered to Mr. Murray as sets of tee-shirts and rugby shorts were produced. "Are you sure I have enough money to pay for it?"

Mr. Murray smiled. "Relax, Thad. Mr. White can afford it, even if you can't. Besides, the first time is always the worst. After this, you'll only have to replace stuff as you grow out of it. Just be grateful that Gran looked after the rest of your clothes."

I wasn't convinced. I'd never seen so many clothes for one person in my life. I'd seen mounds of clothes before. At Wahmurra we got a new shirt and pair of trousers twice a year, and when they were being handed out, the storeroom's mounds looked as high as those on the counter. The only difference was that these were all for me.

While I frowned at the hoard in front of me, wondering if I'd ever wear all of it, one of the ladies extracted a pair of shorts and a shirt from a pile. "Here," she said, "Change into these, while I sew your hatband onto the boater. You'd better put your shoes and socks on now as well."

When Mr. Graham arrived, I was glad I'd changed. My new leather shoes felt uncomfortable but, hopefully, they'd soften after a couple of weeks. I needed my crutches, but I was able to stand straight while my new housemaster scrutinized me.

Apparently I passed muster, because Mr. Graham smiled and held out his hand. "We're going to enjoy having you, Thad. Your room's ready. Now, what say we haul this stuff over there now, and you can unpack it and have everything ready for when you come back on Sunday?"

As Mr. Graham led the way along a wide bushland trail lined with wattles and red banksias, he chatted about school events with Mr. Murray, only stopping when they reached a dignified older building. "This is School House. It was the original family's mansion and became the foundation of the school when we moved here in 1929. There were even classrooms in it for a while."

School House was a brick building set amongst towering eucalyptus trees and flowering shrubs. The house looked like an architectural nightmare. I wondered if the architect had got drunk one night and bet someone about the number of corbels, turrets, gables and arches he could put into it. The bricks, though, were interesting. I figured they were a hundred years old. They had more precise edges than the ones we'd made at Wahmurra, and they had the patina of age.

When Mr. Graham opened the door to my room, I couldn't believe it. It was easily two or three times the size of Chloe's room in Dakin House, and seemed too large for only two boys. Three armchairs were grouped around a fireplace; there were separate desks, and a doorway led to a private bathroom. Mr. Graham pointed to the bed next to a bay window and told me this was mine.

I wanted to turn my music as high as it would go and dance. Somehow Mr. White had got me a room I could escape to, a sanctuary and, even if the roommate should be a problem, there was enough space to ignore him.

"It's magnificent, just like a hotel. We certainly didn't have anything like this in my day," Mr. Murray said.

"Actually, you did. This used to be part of the old headmaster's suite," Mr. Graham informed them. "Now, we just keep it ready for VIPs."

"V.I.P.s? At a school?" Mr. Murray scoffed.

"Don't laugh," Mr. Graham told him. "Only about ten years ago, a young prince and his bodyguard boarded in this room. Boys who take the room understand that the school can reassign them at any time, and they have to be willing to get out at a moment's notice. Thad, I can't tell you how happy you've made young Peters by being willing to share."

More Mr. White. I hadn't known a thing. But Mr. Graham's face looked troubled when he said, "It's too bad Jones didn't wait while we contacted you. He's something of a snob. He heard some gossip about the Trust and a scholarship, put two and two together and made twenty-nine. He's outraged by the fact that he had to move for what he calls a 'charity case.' His father complained to Dr. Rivers. Won't they be surprised when they find out who you are? That you're the school's biggest V.I.P ever?"

Mr. Graham thankfully seemed to run out of breath. Maybe the mounds of clothes waiting to go into drawers took his breath away. He huffed for a few moments before continuing. "Now, Mr. Murray, I'll just show Thad the way to the dining hall and the junior common room. Then, he's set to go."

"And I must see if Mr. White's finished with Dr. Rivers," Mr. Murray said and left as well.

By the time I got back to the room my leg ached. As did my ears. Mr. Graham was a font of information and he insisted on passing it on. I was so sick of history lessons and explanations. I just wanted to stretch out on my comfortable-looking bed, but a bell sounded, and Mr. Graham almost raced across the room towards the door. "That's the end of school. I have to get back to my class and dismiss it. When you finish unpacking, just wait outside for Mr. Murray. He won't be able to get back in without a key card."

I emptied the remaining bags from the store and looked around more carefully. The wall opposite my bed was covered with posters of cricketers. Photos and a computer adorned my roommate's desk, so much so that it stopped a tad short of being messy. My side of the room looked stark and unwelcoming. Maybe I could get pictures of Wahmurra from Mr. White, and I knew Chloe and Mr. Murray would give me stuff. The cricket posters I could do without.

I put the silk tie into my backpack, together with a white shirt to wear back with my suit after the weekend and shrugged it over my shoulders. Then I remembered the silly boater and shoved it on.

I balanced on my crutches just as the front door opened suddenly and slammed into me. A horde of boys came storming through, one politely stopping to hold the door open. I was halfway through the entrance when someone pushed me from behind and I fell hard to the ground half in and out of the doorway.

"Look, Jonesy. There's the charity case you had to move for. Too bad he's a crip. Guess that's why he needed a room on the ground floor."

I recognized the faces looking down at me. Not that I could name them, of course, but I'd seen their like before. They would have been the ones toadying up to Ol' Bundy. By themselves they weren't cruel. In a pack though, they became bullies. Jonesy seemed to be their leader. He was good-looking and seemed a year or so older than me and a good half head taller than everyone else. He was enjoying himself. His smile was arrogant, self-assured, like he knew how this scene would end.

I knew that the next few minutes determined my future at King William's School for Boys. I grabbed my crutches, tried to stand, but fell when pushed again from behind.

Jonesy's friends roared with laughter. The boy who was still holding the door open looked angry. I felt humiliated as I sat on the ground, blocking the entrance to

School House. More and more students arrived and, behind them, Mr. Murray looked like he wanted to come in and brawl with Jonesy and his goons.

The only good thing I could think of was that Chloe was still at Enderby. Otherwise, she'd be running into the middle of things, fists flying, and I'd have no reputation at all.

Just when I felt the most alone, the boy who'd been holding the door open came over and held his hand out to pull me up. I had a friend, whoever he was. I smiled and waved the offer off, but he stayed by me, his hands fisted.

Then I swiveled round to face Jonesy. "Look, I'm sorry you felt you had to leave your room. It wasn't my choice." When there was no response, I raised my voice. "I know what we should do is find a place and go at it. One on one. But we can't. We're not allowed. In any case, I can't stand on my own two feet right now, much less fight on them," I said with the slight grin that I hoped would disarm him.

There was no answering smile from Jonesy, no hint really that he'd heard anything I said. I sat on the ground, humiliated, until I realized there was one thing I could challenge him to. I was still polite, but I hope there was frost in my voice when I said, "There's something I know I can do right now—and that's rowing. So, Jonesy, I challenge you to a race. Any time. Any distance."

I knew something was wrong when I heard snickers in the crowd. "You're challenging me to a rowing race, charity boy? Don't you even know who I am?" Jonesy's cruel smile destroyed the beauty of his face.

I shrugged. He might be the school bully, but he wasn't Ol' Bundy. This time I didn't care if I sounded polite or not. "You're probably someone who pulled the wings off insects when you were a kid. To me, you're just a jerk who knocks people down. Being in a boat should even things up."

"Why won't you man up and fight?"

"Besides what I just said about not being able to stand up? Well, I promised Dr. Rivers an hour ago to obey the school rules. I may look crippled," I went on, sending a scathing look at Jonesy's friends, "but I keep my word."

Jonesy's friends erupted again. "Hear that? He's pi, Jonesy! Well, crip, pious doesn't cut it here. That's not why he's not fighting you, Jonesy. He's scared you'll beat him to a pulp."

Jonesy left the group and walked slowly over to stand in front of me like he had every power in the world. "Just for your information, little boy, I'm the junior rowing champ. So, what are you going to do when I thrash your sorry ass on the river? Run to Mommy?"

I looked at him. "That's all you got? Seriously?" Slowly, like a male stripper, I shrugged off my backpack and unbuttoned my shirt. With everyone mesmerized, I took it off slowly. Then I twisted around. "Look my back, Jonesy. What makes you think you can do anything worse to me than what's been done already."

There was dead silence. Chloe had once said that the ridges and furrows on my back, the legacy of my flogging, reminded her of a waffle. From the silence, I knew none had ever seen a whipped back before, much less one that had survived a cat-o-nine-tails.

I put my shirt back on, picked up my crutches, then hooked one of them between Jonesy's legs and tugged. As he toppled to the ground, I knew I'd always cherish his look of total surprise.

I would never have thought there were degrees of silence, but, impossibly, the doorway became totally quiet. No one seemed to even breathe as I looked at Jonesy.

"Now, we're even."

As I pulled myself up, two boys moved. The one who'd held the door open picked my backpack up and dusted it off. The other, obviously a senior, judging from his size and air of command, shouldered his way through the crowd and offered his hand.

"I'm Luke Morriset. Captain of the house. Would someone care to tell me what's going on?"

"I'm Thaddeus Compton." I heard reactions to the sound of my name and understood what Dr. Rivers meant. Thaddeus Compton was a name the school knew. "I'm new. So new that my shoes can't grip the polished floor and I fell."

Luke Morriset wasn't buying the explanation. "And?" he said in a voice that was used to being answered.

"And Jonesy and I were discussing a rowing race."

Luke now looked very interested. "A rowing race? Well, isn't that amazing? As captain of rowing, I'll have no trouble organizing it. How about Wednesday morning? Jones, you understand?"

After Jonesy nodded, Luke sort of looked over my head. "Well, Thaddeus Compton," he began, sounding every syllable in my name as though he wanted to make sure every Dubbee got it, "I've just been briefed about you. Button your shirt up, put your tie on, and brush the dirt off. Your dad's waiting for you, and you can't go out in public looking half-dressed. By the way, welcome to King William's and School House. As for the rest of you? Follow me. I want a word."

10

"So, I'm your father now, in addition to my other sins," Mr. Murray commented as we walked to the huge traffic circle that served at the school's drop-off point.

I tried to read his face. "I just wanted to get out of there. I didn't want to contradict Luke, and it was too complicated to explain."

"I agree. Now, here's Jim with the Rolls. In you get."

As we drove towards Enderby, Mr. Murray asked, "What was going on back there? I thought helping would have been the kiss of death, so I stayed out of it. You handled yourself well, Thad. Good job."

I blushed. Mr. Murray's praise was almost as rare as Mr. White's, and I respected him for not interfering. "Jonesy resents me because he had to move out of the room. At least, I think that's how things started. But I also think he likes picking on people who can't fight back, and I can't. Not for a while, anyway. So, I challenged him to a rowing race."

Mr. Murray seemed to think for a moment. "What happens when you lose?"

"You mean when I win, don't you?"

"Thad, you have to realize that boats have changed a lot over the years."

"I haven't. I was a good rower in 1833 and just as good now. I think, anyway."

Mr. Murray laughed. "You're going to do really well at King William's, Thad. I'm glad Chloe brought you to our time so I could meet you."

I blushed again. Fortunately the car turned into Enderby's traffic circle and Chloe waved at us. She stuffed her pack into the back, whipped her panama off, and took a long look at me in my new school clothes. "Well, well, well," she grinned and tipped my boater off my head and put it on hers. "Do I look gorgeous or what?"

"It's good to see you too," Mr. Murray said in a quiet voice.

Chloe settled immediately. "Sorry, Dad. It's just that I've looked forward to this for so long, wondering how Thad would look in his Dubbee's uniform. He looks great though, doesn't he?"

"It's good to see you too," I said, echoing the tone in Mr. Murray's voice.

She hugged me, ignored my surprise, and turned back to her father. "Dad, I'm starved. Can we eat somewhere around here before we go home? Then we won't have to drive through peak hour traffic."

Mr. Murray pulled his phone out. "I'll check with Mr. White. It will depend when he wants his car back."

After Mr. Murray reported that Mr. White would stay overnight in Dr. Rivers' house, Chloe asked, "Dad, can we go to Michael Dee's? Everyone says it's great."

"Do you say it's great, Thad?" When I shook my head, Mr. Murray smiled. "I don't either. Well, you see, Chloe, not everyone thinks that. But, if it means so much that you've forgotten all the manners we've tried to teach you, by all means. Let's eat at Michael Dee's."

Although it was quite early, the parking lot was jammed. People stared as Mr. White's antique Rolls circled slowly before it stopped at the restaurant's entrance. I got out, balanced on my crutches, held the door open for Chloe. She plunked my boater on my head. "Remember, Dubbee, you've got to wear this in public. And that means the five steps from the car into the restaurant. Strange, but fact."

I grimaced. It made zero sense, but then she plopped her own school hat on. I'd never imagined such silly rules, but when we hung them up there were about thirty others. Four had the green and maroon stripes of King William's.

Michael Dee's had a menu designed for adolescents, especially those pining for something different after weeks on school food. While Mr. Murray ordered a drink, I read the menu from cover to cover. No Balmain Bugs, but there were twenty-seven kinds of pizzas.

How was I supposed to choose? I started going e*enie, meenie*, etc. and then ordered what my finger landed on—feta cheese and artichoke.

After the server bustled away, Mr. Murray and Chloe burst out laughing. "Do you have any idea what you've just ordered?" Chloe asked. "I bet you've never eaten an artichoke in your life."

I shrugged. "There's always a first time." While she talked to her dad, I looked around the restaurant, recognized a face in the distance and asked Mr. Murray if a friend could join us. Chloe's eyebrows went up, and I knew I had finally surprised her.

"How can you say that? You don't know anyone." She glared at the tables around us, and I decided to keep her curiosity unanswered.

Mr. Murray looked like he wanted to laugh. "Go ahead, Thad. There's plenty of room in the booth."

I was tired by the time I struggled my way across to a small table in the far corner. "Hi," I began, my arms trembling with the effort to stand straight. "I'm Thad Compton. Thanks for being willing to fight Jonesy and his friends with me."

A boy, roughly the same size as me, stood and held his hand out. "Matt Peters. And this is my mother. Mom, this is Thad, the boy I was telling you about." After I'd shaken hands with Mrs. Peters, Matt dropped a minor bombshell. "In addition to everything, I'm also your roommate. I'm glad you came and got rid of Jonesy."

I smiled, knowing that life at King William's had just become manageable. Matt looked like he loved to laugh. His coppery brown hair had a cowlick that made it fall forward, his eyes were friendly, and I already knew I could count on him in a crunch. "Great. Look, would you like to join us, Mrs. Peters? We've got plenty of room."

After I introduced them and they had settled, Matt turned towards Thad. "Thad, you won't know this, but you've made a major enemy with Jonesy."

Chloe, of course, looked interested. "Jonesy? An enemy already? You were only there an hour."

Matt grimaced, almost as though he knew what sisters were like. He sent me an apologetic look and briefly explained what had happened. Chloe laughed when Matt explained how I'd upended Jonesy. "I wished I'd seen that." Then she frowned. "Thad, if Jonesy is who I think he is, Matt's right. You'll have to be careful. Matt, is he Bruce Jones?"

Matt laughed. "Oh, yes. Thad, if you ever want to get him furious, just call him Bruce. He hates it. Seriously though, look out for him. He's been bigger and stronger than any of us since he first came to the school. He's been shaving for donkey's years."

I couldn't help myself. I rubbed the back of my hand against my chin. Almost. Then I tuned back into what Matt was saying, "He brags that he's been having sex for a couple of years, and that seems to make him feel like he's more male than we are. Plus, he's got a real mean streak. He'll try to get you when you're not looking. Just watch your back. All the time, Thad. Every second, every minute. All the time."

I shrugged. Jonesy could never be worse than Ol' Bundy's bunch at Wahmurra. Before I could say anything though, the waiter arrived with our meals. When I looked down at mine, I felt horrified and I totally got why Chloe and her dad had laughed.

Chloe, of course, couldn't leave it alone. "Told you."

"You're a vegetarian?" Matt's voice cracked with disbelief, as he too looked at the feta cheese and artichoke toppings. "You'd better make sure Jonesy never finds out."

In all the excitement, I'd forgotten about Billy's message until I woke on Saturday morning. Then I couldn't wait to see what lay behind the boathouse wall. I dressed quickly and walked along to Chloe's door and knocked. "Hurry. Get dressed. Let's find out what Billy left us."

Although I nearly slipped on the dewy grass, I managed to keep myself upright as I hobbled down the stairs to the sea wall. It was low tide, and the sand looked dirty. The wash of the incoming tide played with a mangled tire so that it drifted one way and then the other. Not everything adapted easily. It might take years before the tire broke up or became imbedded in the sand and a habitat for sea life.

I so desperately hoped I wouldn't be like the tire, just tossed around with no say in what happened to me.

"What are you looking at?" Chloe called as she ran down the stairs.

Picking up my crutches, I hobbled over to the boathouse. It seemed smaller than I remembered from 1833. "Is it me?" I asked Chloe. "It used to be bigger, didn't it?"

"Yes. Some of it fell down ages ago, and Gran's

father knocked more down when he fixed it up," Chloe said as she opened the door. "Anyway, I think I remember Gran saying that the old one was bigger."

I half expected to find cobwebs and dust everywhere, but I hadn't reckoned on Mr. Murray. Coils of rope hung from hooks, tools were in wall niches, and an old sail stretched across the rafters added a touch of whimsy.

Carefully balancing, I bent down and peered at the wall, counted, then pushed and tugged at the fifth stone from the bottom and from the door. "Billy says the package is here, but this isn't loose. It's cemented tightly to the others. I've pushed, but nothing happens."

Chloe squatted between a slip rail and the door to Gran's prized rose garden. "Um, it looks like it's been caulked."

I felt my shoulders slump. "Does that mean that someone's been here already? Ol' Bundy?"

"Thad, how can I get through to you that Ol' Bundy is dead? He couldn't have come through your thumbprint in that old brick. It's just not possible. You've tried. Mom tried. It only works for me. In any case, if any Bundy had been here, it would be Frank, and he'd have plastered what he found all over *Gotta Know*."

I nodded, and once she saw I wasn't going to argue with her, she went on, "Anyway, let's not tie ourselves into knots. I'll get some tools and we'll see."

I thought our chances of finding what Billy left were almost zero. The caulking looked so new. Wouldn't whoever had done the caulking have looked behind the stone? "Do you think Billy meant the old wall? The one that fell down?"

"Can't have. His package would have been found when they cleaned the mess away. And, don't forget, the time Billy's talking about, the time he says he saw you in, has to be somewhere in the future. You haven't worn that striped tie yet or earned the green and maroon jacket." She got to her feet and leaned on the work bench. "It's strange that Billy knows so much about us, and I just know him as a five year old."

"A naughty five year old," I said with a smile, remembering some of Billy and Polly's escapades.

"A naughty pair of five year olds," Chloe agreed. "I don't think I ever saw Polly with a clean dress after nine o'clock in the morning." She pulled a drawer open and began rummaging. "Dad's got some tools here, somewhere. Let's see what they do."

Seconds later with a triumphant smile, she produced a chisel and a hammer. "Ta-da. I'll hold the chisel. You hammer and see if anything happens. You're dead if you miss and get my fingers, though."

No way. I wasn't going to risk death. I grabbed the chisel and began tapping around the stone. Chloe swung the hammer as though it were a tennis racquet and hit her knuckles against the wall. "Ow."

I took the hammer from her and resumed my careful exploration. "Here. Feel this bit here. It's really soft." I hit the chisel a little harder, and it slipped between the fourth and fifth stones. After working for a few moments, the stone loosened, and we leveraged it free and carefully placed it on the ground. "Now, Billy," I whispered, "Let's see what this is all about."

"Wait a moment," Chloe said, grabbing hold of an old coat hanger. She untwisted the handle part and handed it over. "Best check for spiders before you go fishing."

I worked until the hanger was reasonably straight and then poked it around the cavity, hoping to destroy cobwebs and hungry tarantula spiders. Then I swallowed and put my arm into the cavity. No matter how hard I tried, and I even hoisted myself onto a ledge and tried from there, I couldn't reach the bottom.

"I can't do it," I admitted eventually. "I can't get my balance. See if you can reach it."

Of course, she could. I felt a little humiliated when she carefully extracted a tightly bound package. She handed it over, but after working on the string knots for a few minutes, I handed it back. "Can you do it? You've got longer fingernails."

"Seems useless to try. Let's get a knife," she suggested.

When I unwrapped the canvas-covered package a few minutes later in the kitchen, I struggled hard not to break down and sob. Billy had sent a couple of daguerreotypes, the forerunners of photographs. In the first, he stood, arm in arm, with a friend. They wore top hats, striped waistcoats and long sideburns and looked very pleased with themselves. The inscription read: "Billy Kendricks and Luc Morriset, upon graduation from Oxford." The second, not as faded as the first, showed an older Billy sitting with a baby in a long christening robe. On the back, Billy had written, "William Peter Kendricks, aged three months."

I handed them across to Chloe without saying anything and knuckled tears back. Billy had gone to England and then come back to Australia to raise a family. What happened to that family? Why weren't they at Wahmurra? By rights it should be Kendricks property, not Mr. White's.

When Chloe looked up, her face was sad as well. "He looks like he grew up to be a nice person. I'll always remember him being five and saying 'dissembling' all the time. But, what courage he had, Thad! Remember when he told that officer off in the work yard?"

I remembered. I'd never forget, no matter what century I was in. When Chloe had come storming down to break up my flogging, Billy had followed her and told the officer that, in the absence of both his father and Mr. White, he was in charge of Wahmurra, not the officer. Then, he ordered the whipping stopped until one of them returned. Billy had guts.

"What's this? Another letter?" Chloe asked, breaking into my thoughts and pointing to a couple of folded pieces of paper.

I picked it up and groaned when I saw pages of numbers. "It's another cipher, and I've left the key at school."

"Can't we work it out again? We can look it up on Google. I'll help."

My stomach rumbled. "After we've eaten," I told her. "It will take a while."

Mr. Murray joined us for breakfast and, after he'd seen the photos, was easily persuaded to postpone a planned sail until the afternoon. He offered to help, but I told him it was really a two-person job. While Chloe searched for the Athanasian Creed, I wrote the numbers 1 through 275. The deciphering went easier this time, and then our mouths dropped open.

HELLO, THAD. I HAVE PUT MY DIARY AND OTHER NON-SECRET INFORMATION INTO ONE BIG ENVELOPE. I AM LEAVING IT IN THE KING WILLIAM'S LIBRARY WITH INSTRUCTIONS THAT IT BE KEPT UNTIL YOU ASK FOR IT. I'VE ALSO LEFT FOUR PACKAGES WHERE I GUESSED YOU MIGHT FIND THEM, BECAUSE I WANT YOU TO KNOW THAT THERE ARE AT LEAST THREE DOORWAYS BETWEEN OUR WORLDS. THREE, BESIDES THE YELLOW BRICK THAT ONLY CHLOE CAN USE. I THINK EVERYONE HAS THEIR OWN DOOR. I COULD NOT GET THROUGH CHLOE'S, AND POLLY CANNOT USE THE BRICK OR MINE IN THE BOAT HOUSE. GOOD

LUCK, THAD. USE THE GIFTS WISELY.
BILLY.

"Use," Chloe said immediately. "He said use, not used. That must mean that I go back to their time at some stage. I wonder why he's so insistent that you know there's more than one doorway."

The first sentence though had captured my attention. "I can't wait to get back to school to see what's in the library. Maybe there will be an old photo of Lord and Lady Peter. Gran would like that, I think."

"Dad, too," Chloe added softly.

11

I didn't want to go rowing on Monday morning. I wanted to go to the library and see what else Billy had left. But Mr. Murray's words when he dropped me off for chapel had been ominous, "Don't screw up, Thad. Until you know your way around, just keep the rules, and stay out of trouble."

So grudgingly I got up when it was still dark. I apologized to Matt when I woke him up, but he mumbled something about being used to Jonesy and went back to sleep. I put on my brand new trainers, hobbled over to the dining hall, then to the bus. When Luke Morriset checked me onto to it, something struck me.

Billy's friend was Luc Morriset. Was he this Luke's ancestor? It was a question without an answer. Like all the unanswered Mr. White ones I'd stored away in my memory.

When the bus stopped at the school's rowing complex, everyone raced off to a central building, and I had no idea whether I should follow them or not. Dr. Rivers said I'd be rowing, so I walked down to the water's edge and then stopped with my mouth half open.

Tied up to the dock was a brand new boat. It was one of the new-fangled long skinny ones, but my, oh my, it was beautiful. Even better, it had my name on it. More of Mr. White's magic I supposed as I levered myself into it.

Moments later I was out in the middle of the Hawkesbury River and shouting for joy. Clumps of mist waited for the sun to vaporize them, and the concentric ripples made by fish gulping flies widened until they became indistinguishable. Congregations of herons hovered in the mangroves, staring at the ripples with hopeful concentration. Currawongs trilled, and a kookaburra flashed downwards towards an unsuspecting fish.

It was a regular cornucopia of beautiful things—except for the commuter train trundling its way towards Sydney on the bridge behind me.

The boat's seat moved forward and back when I rowed, and I didn't know if I liked that. Even the oars were different with oblong blades attached to them at an odd angle. So far, I'd caught more air than river, and I drenched myself every time I managed to get a decent pull through the water.

I didn't care. As time went by, I smacked the oars against the river in happiness. Finally, everything felt right.

Sometimes I let the boat drift in the river. At other times I pulled hard with those funny oars. I knew I'd ache tomorrow, but it was worth it. My boat had the look and smell of new things. A plastic new thing, not wood. It truly was beautiful.

I remembered seeing boats like this from the summer when we'd driven to Wahmurra in Mr. White's Rolls. I'd wondered then what it would feel like to row one; now, I knew. Tippy, but it seemed to sense when and what I wanted to do. It was like riding a horse again.

"Compton! Oy!"

The shout came from upriver. I recognized Jonesy's voice and wondered why he sounded so gleeful.

"Compton!" he yelled again from a similar boat to mine about twenty yards away. "Coach wants to see you. Take your time. No hurry."

"What for?"

"You'll find out." Jonesy began turning his boat

around. "By the way, you wanted a race. How about now?"

I looked back at the King William's dock and saw a man staring downriver at me. I sensed impatience and knew, from what my guts sensed and from what Matt had told me, that Jonesy was trying to get me in trouble.

Immediately, clumsily, I turned to row back. But the boat felt unfamiliar and difficult. I couldn't find a rhythm. The oars refused to cooperate, and I managed to get even more of the river onto myself. Worse, even with my best effort, I only managed to make up five yards on Jonesy. My legs just weren't strong enough. By the time I reached the dock, he'd secured his boat and stood with a group of his friends, waiting like vultures for something to happen.

"Over here!"

I tried my best to get out of the boat. The leg I needed to support myself was my weak one, and someone had taken my crutches away. I scanned the dock, looking for something to hold onto. It was a hive of busyness with rowers taking boats from the shed and carrying them to the water. Then I saw my crutches, perched precariously on a post near Jonesy and his friends.

I'd rarely felt this helpless. I tried my best to get out of the boat again but, of course, my weak leg buckled. Again, and again. Grabbing hold of the dock only gave a new meaning to futility. Matt had been dead right when he'd warned me against Jonesy. He exuded malice. So far, his tricks were embarrassing but relatively harmless. What would happen when he became seriously angry? Like, for instance, when I beat him in the race?

Luke Morriset, who had been checking something off on a clipboard, finally realized what was wrong. He walked across to Jonesy, said something which I couldn't hear, grabbed my crutches, and walked back to the edge of the dock.

"Here, do you want these or would it be better if I pulled you up?"

"Pull me up, I think. Then the crutches. Thanks."

As I struggled across the uneven wooden dock to the man I assumed was the coach, I felt less worried with Luke beside me. He steadied me more than once when the crutches slipped on the wet wood. I was even more grateful when I saw that the coach's face was as red as a boiled lobster.

"Who are you?" the coach stormed. "What made you think you had any right to take my brand new shell?"

Luke tried reassurance. "Coach," he said, "Thad enrolled only last Friday. He's been in hospital recovering from surgery on his leg, and his doctors thought rowing would help him get better. I'm sure Dr. Rivers sent you a message."

The coach grunted. "Too busy to look at messages." But he sounded calmer as he looked at me again and asked, "I don't care who you are, or that you're new. What in the blazes made you think you could waltz in here and take out my new shell without checking with me first?"

I must have looked like a dead fish. I knew something was wrong, but I couldn't figure out what. "I didn't know that I had to check in, sir. I just saw the boat with my name on it, and assumed it was what I was supposed to use."

"Shell," Coach interrupted.

"Shell," I repeated.

"New boys don't get new shells. You must know that. So, what made you think you could waltz in here and go off in my brand new shell?"

"I've just told you. Once I saw its name, I thought I could use it."

Out of the corner of my eye I could see Jonesy in hearing distance. Had he somehow set this up to get me into trouble? Obviously, the new shell was a prized possession. But why did it have my name on it if I wasn't supposed to use it?

As Coach's face got redder, Jonesy's grin grew wider. For several long moments, there was a stalemate. Then Luke laughed. "Coach. There really is a simple explanation. Forgive me for not introducing Thad properly. His full name is Thaddeus Compton."

Everyone turned and stared at the maroon lettering on the side of new shell—*Thaddeus Compton*.

Coach exploded. "He's Thaddeus Compton? Of the Compton Trust? He's that Thaddeus Compton?"

Luke nodded. "And the Compton Trust, as you know, is King William's Rowing Club's official sponsor."

Now I looked horrified. "I thought the cricket oval was bad enough. This is worse."

Coach stared at me, at the lettering on the shell, and then nodded. "I understand. Famous ancestors can be difficult to live up to. You must always remember that, Thad." He stared at Thad again, and his voice became plummy when he continued, "'It is indeed a desirable thing to be well descended….'"

"'But the glory belongs to our ancestors.'" I finished. "Plutarch, sir."

"A classicist," Coach murmured, while Luke looked at me in astonishment.

I flushed. "Sorry. I didn't mean to show off. It's just that my old tutor used to say half of a quotation and expect me to know the other part."

Coach surveyed his various crews on the water before continuing. "Tell me about your rowing. What on earth were you doing out there? Trying to get half the river in my new shell?"

I fiddled with my crutches, trying to work out what to

say. "I was enjoying myself, sir. I've been cooped up in hospitals forever. It felt so good to get out on the river. I didn't mean to break any rules."

"Um." Coach didn't sound convinced, but his voice sharpened when he continued. "Well, I can't say I blame you for that. Tell me where you learned to row. Who taught you?"

I looked at him in surprise and, again, didn't quite know how to answer. "No one. I taught myself."

Jonesy and his friends snickered. Bad move. Coach suddenly remembered them. "Jones," he shouted. "Over here." When Jonesy appeared, Coach looked at us. "Luke tells me you two are going to race on Wednesday. Is that right?"

Jonesy smiled. "We're going to be on the water at the same time, Coach. Don't expect it to be much of a race."

"What's the distance?"

"I think it should be five hundred meters. After all, Compton's just out of hospital. I don't want to tire him out and send him back into it, Coach."

I wished I was strong enough to punch the smirk off Jonesy's face, particularly when Coach said, "Leave everything to me. I'll organize it. Jones, get yourself out on the river and don't waste more time. Thad, come with me."

Coach officially enrolled me as a member of the rowing club and then began to explain how I could get more power when I rowed. "You've got a brave heart, boy. I watched you make up time on Jonesy. I'll give you an old boat tomorrow. The new shell's actually for Luke. He's our senior champion. So, don't take offense. And, on Wednesday, give a good account of yourself. Try your best. There's no shame if you do that."

12

I expected to be able to go to the library after school to see what Billy had left, but Mr. Graham waited for me when English ended and took me to a study booth. After I sat down, he produced a package of tests.

I'd never seen anything like them. At first, I thought they were for dunces. Every question had a choice of answers that were actually helpful. However when Mr. Graham produced the mathematics test, I wanted to cry. I didn't know the answer to the first question. Worse, I couldn't even guess it.

I'd never seen mathematics like these before, so I did the most logical thing. I said *eenie, meenie, miney, mo* and chose whatever box the rhyme ended on. The next test was word puzzles. Most were easy and, again with the help of *eenie, meenie*, I finished them quickly.

Mr. Graham said he would be back in two hours. That left thirty minutes time, and I wondered what to do. I felt frustrated, partly because the tests hadn't covered the subjects I was really good at. I'd never had trouble with school before, and I wanted to prove to Mr. Murray that I was worth whatever King William's cost.

Finally I figured out what to do—an essay. I wrote the reason for it in Latin, and then I described my feelings of uselessness in ancient Greek. When Mr. Graham opened the door, I nearly jumped out of my skin. He picked up the essay, blinked, and looked at it again. "What's this, Thad?"

"I didn't know a lot of stuff, sir. I finished early and, rather than just sit here, I wrote down why I couldn't answer anything. I don't want people to think I'm stupid."

"I see," Mr. Graham murmured, frowning as he looked at the page of symbols in front of him. "But Thad, what language have you explained this in?"

"Greek, sir."

Mr. Graham still looked bemused as he walked off in the direction of Dr. Rivers' office. "If you hurry off now, you'll have just enough time to change for dinner," he called back to me.

"What have you been doing?" Matt asked as soon as I walked in. "I looked for you everywhere after cricket practice."

While I changed into my casual clothes, I told Matt what had happened. He looked puzzled by the story of the Greek essay. "Do you mean you truly didn't know any of the answers?" After I nodded, he went on, "Anyway, don't worry about that now. I've got news. I'm coming to your race on Wednesday."

"You are? How? You're not a rower?"

"I asked Luke if I could be your manager for the race," he answered looking smug. "You need someone to watch your back if Jonesy's involved. Anyway, I asked first and got the job. Everyone's trying to think of ways to watch. Hasan offered to pay $10 for the bus ride. There's talk that they'll send an extra bus."

"Why? Why would anyone want to drag themselves out of bed at the crack of dawn when they don't have to?"

"There's a lot of betting on the race. Jonesy and his mates started it by giving outrageous odds—fifty to one. Everyone's gone crazy. And," Matt said as we left for the dining hall, "as well, everyone wants to be there in case you beat Jonesy. I bet Kyle Beresford right at the beginning before they dropped the odds. I've got $20 on you."

I didn't know what to say and, for the rest of the night, I stayed right by Matt. Boys I'd never met came up and wished me good luck. I felt harassed. At the river, the next morning, Coach asked me to stay behind. "Take this scull out today," he said. "I can't offer any coaching. Best preparation is probably what you did yesterday. Go out now and enjoy yourself."

I felt glad I'd followed Coach's advice when I got back to school. Mr. Graham met the bus, escorted me to Dr. Rivers' office, and then left. At first I thought I was in trouble because of the race. Then I saw my tests in Dr. Rivers' hand when he came in. After we shook hands, I grimaced. "I didn't do well, did I?"

"I don't think we can say that, Thad," he said slowly. "As you might guess, you did exceptionally badly on the mathematics section. In fact, I doubt if any boy in Year 5 could do worse."

Year 5. I'd expected Year 1. "I've never been taught anything like that."

He didn't seem too perturbed. "There was a revolution in mathematical thinking in the last century. Not to worry, though. We'll tutor you and get you up to speed in no time. You seem to understand the basics. No, that's not why I asked you here. By and large, your English is good, and you'll have to work hard to keep up with your class in History and Geography. However, I faxed your Greek essay over to a friend last night, and he's very excited."

"Fax, sir?"

After explaining it to me, Dr. Rivers went on, "He's a Classics professor at Macquarie University. He's never heard of anyone as fluent as you at your age. In fact, he says you have a total range of expressions that are new to him. More than that, you're at university level. He's offered to give you a seminar twice a week. You'll get first year credit, I believe."

I didn't know what that meant and didn't much care. I loved Greek, and all I understood was that I'd be tutored in it again. "And Latin? Will he teach me that?"

"No, we'll do that here. Now, this is what I'm proposing. We'll keep your afternoon classes as they are, but you'll go to Macquarie University for Greek on Tuesday and Thursday mornings. One of our retired teachers lives close by, and he's willing to pick you up and tutor you in mathematics. You'll go to the university by taxi and come back with him. Deal?"

I'm sure my smile showed how happy I was. I'd thought I'd have to go to math classes with boys in kindergarten. As I started fumbling with my crutches, Dr. Rivers added softly, "Thad? About the race? Fight hard."

By bedtime, I wished I'd challenged Jonesy to a game of tiddlywinks. Everyone had an opinion. Some favored Jonesy, but a huge majority wished me good luck. "I don't think Jonesy knows how unpopular he is," I told Matt as we flossed our teeth.

Matt smiled. "I don't think he cares. I'm even more astonished that Beresford and his mob don't have any idea they'll be bankrupt by the time school starts tomorrow. You are going to win, aren't you?"

The truth was I didn't know. The racing shells were so different from what I was used to. Jonesy had surprised me, and I knew why he was so cocky about the race. But when I saw the Hawkesbury the following morning, I began to believe I'd have a real chance. White-capped waves raced towards the Pacific Ocean, and a blustery wind pinned the mangroves low towards the water.

Calm, placid water would have favored Jonesy. Seagulls surfing air currents made things even.

"Where are we going?" I whispered to Matt when Coach bundled us, Jonesy, Kyle Beresford, Luke and some senior boys into a power boat.

"The starting station's down river. All the races start there. Don't worry, Thad. I've got your back."

I'd felt such responsibility only once before. That was back when a thug shot Chloe. Looking after Billy and Polly Kendricks seemed dreamtime in comparison to being the focus of so much betting. Matt, for example, didn't have much money. Yet, in blind faith, or the hope of revenge on Jonesy, he'd gambled $20 on me.

We reached the starting station—a narrow structure in the river with nine slots for boats. Two black dinghies bobbed in the middle slips and, once he saw them, Jonesy began shouting. "Coach, where's my scull? You can't seriously expect me to race in this."

"I've evened the odds, Jones. You'll row in dinghies, because Thad hasn't had much experience with sculls. However, I've also taken your training in account as well, so the distance will be two thousand meters. That way I've rewarded your experience."

The metric system was like the new mathematics—incomprehensible. But as far as I could work out, it was almost two miles. Eminently doable, if I had two strong legs. One strong leg? I could only try.

Jonesy, though, was stamping his feet as he tried to change Coach's mind. "It's a joke," he shouted. "Thad's leg is too weak for that distance. It should be five hundred, at the most."

"And, of course, Jonesy's a sprinter. Five hundred is his best race," Matt commented semi-audibly.

While Jonesy argued, Luke and another rower went to

the fourth and fifth slots, untied two aluminum dinghies, then stretched out, anchoring the boats with their fingers. "Ready, Coach," Luke called over.

Matt helped me into the dinghy in the fifth slot. "I'll keep your crutches with me. Watch out for Jonesy. If he thinks Coach isn't watching, he'll try anything. He'll look such a fool if he loses."

As I waited for Jonesy to accept reality, I was glad for the warmth of my new fleecy vest, but Jonesy stripped down, I couldn't believe my eyes. His skintight racing suit didn't leave much to anyone's imagination. If Coach made me wear one of those, I'd join the cricket club.

The dinghy's seat felt uncomfortable but, hallelujah, it didn't slide forward or backward. Plus, the oars were similar to my 1833 ones. If my leg hadn't been restructured, I would have felt confident. As it was, I had absolutely no idea how much strength it had.

I didn't move when the starter's gun fired. I ducked, then looked around, trying to work out who was shooting, and if they were shooting at me.

"Go, go," Matt and Luke shouted. "Row."

Jonesy, already fifteen yards away, looked like a champion. I grabbed my oars, pulled, caught a crab and said several bad words. Then I settled myself and set off after Jonesy. I'd need every bit of my experience on water now to have a chance.

As the waves battered and crashed against the boat, I stroked slowly, feeling out the river and the current. From Matt's frantic shouts, I knew I must look stupid. Obviously, Jonesy thought so too, because his pace slowed.

Keep calm. You have a chance. Then my know-how kicked in, and I let the boat drift in a line towards the north shore of the river.

"Thad, you're going off course," Matt yelled from the

power boat. "Straighten it."

By now, though, I'd found the river current I'd discovered the day before. It cut across the river diagonally, so all I had to do was figure out the right angle to use its strength and get myself back on track.

Jonesy was a speck in the distance, maybe one hundred yards ahead. As I bent my back, and my oars sliced into the current, he decided to play to the crowd. He turned his boat towards the starting station and began to row in slow circles. His back was towards me, so that when my dinghy, propelled by the current, accelerated, I'd almost made up the lead.

He immediately pumped up his stroke rate, but it's hard to get your rhythm back when you've deliberately broken it, and Jonesy found this out the hard way. When he saw that he couldn't lose me, he stroked even faster. But I'd settled into my own rhythm and knew that only my pain threshold could beat me now. My lungs ached as they sought oxygen, every muscle protested and wanted to shut down, and my leg felt like someone had shot a bullet into its muscle mass.

Overall, I felt great.

Although I rowed an oblique line, my course was perfectly straight. I couldn't see Jonesy, but I could hear the ferocity of his oars crashing into the river. Two hundred yards or so to go.

I can do it. I don't care if I have to go back to Greenway, I'm going to win this race and teach that arrogant son-of-a-gun some humility.

Pulling hard through the water, I increased my strokes to an insane pace. I wanted to shout when I passed Jonesy. "Row until you hear the horn," Coach had told me earlier, and that's exactly what I did. When the horn sounded, Jonesy was ten to fifteen yards behind.

When I stopped, a massive cramp seized the muscles in my weak leg, squeezing them until I thought they'd be paper thin. But as I bent over in agony, I heard cheering from the dock.

"Are you all right, Thad?" Matt shouted.

I looked over at Jonesy. He lay back in his boat, obviously knackered. After all, his foolishness had probably added a few hundred yards to his race. I bent forward, picked up my oars, and used up the rest of my energy to row over to the dock. Matt brought my crutches immediately. "How do we get you out?"

"Ask Luke. He knows."

After Luke hauled me out, I really was surprised by the cheers and applause. I didn't know what to do. "Wave your cap," Luke told me. Then he and Matt helped me over to Coach's recovery station, where someone immediately began to massage my leg. By the time Jonesy staggered over, I could even breathe.

I held my hand out to Jonesy. "Good race."

He took my hand for a brief second, then and dropped it like a hot brick. "You only won because I was an idiot. I gave you that race."

Coach came over and, when he said, "Pride goeth before a fall," I realized that he'd always quote because he thought I'd get it. However, he seemed happy and smiled at some hidden joke. "Well, boys," he began. "I like what I saw. The two of you are real competitors, although there's no place for arrogance in a race, Jones."

Jonesy stood. "May I have my shower, sir?"

Coach waved him away. As Jonesy stalked towards the showers, Coach looked at me. "I think I understood what you did out there. Unorthodox, but it worked. Now, young Compton, I have some questions for you. Your style is atrocious, but are you willing to be coached? Will you put in the work that's required to race hard consistently?"

I thought. Did I really want to work hard again? But the agony from the race was already becoming just another memory. "I think so. I don't know how much good I'll be until my leg's better."

"I understand. Believe me, we'll take it easy. We've two months to do it in. The school's just been invited to submit the names of two boys for a newfangled $25,000 race. The key thing is that it's a race for juniors, and that dinghies will be used. No sculls allowed. After this morning, I like our chances. So, we'll begin tomorrow morning, Thad."

On the bus back to school everyone, except me, celebrated. Matt understood. "We'll have to watch Jonesy more than ever. He and his friends lost over a thousand dollars each on the race. Beresford had to tell me he'll pay up in a couple of weeks."

"That's not right," Thad said. "He bet you. He should pay up straightaway. You would have had to."

"He can't," Matt answered. "He has to ask his father, and he's scared what his dad will do to him. I'm telling you, Thad. If I'm not around, watch your back."

13

Chloe's reaction to the race bugged me. Just in case I'd begun to think of myself as a superhero, standing up to bullies around the world, she had news for me. "It was totally dude, macho, mojo," she declared, before adding in her most disparaging voice, "So male."

"You're only upset because you weren't there," I told her.

"True." There was silence on the phone for a nanosecond. "I would kill for the chance to have seen Jonesy's face when he realized he was going to lose. Oh Thad, well, well done."

Her approval felt good, until she asked, "What was in Billy's packet?"

"I don't know."

"You don't know? Why? Is it another code?"

I held my mobile tighter against my ear while I twisted around on my crutches, trying to get comfortable. "I don't know. It's complicated. It's not in the library anymore. It's locked in a vault with some other stuff in the archives here. The archivist's sick, but in any case, I have to make an appointment. Looks like we have to wait till next week."

Chloe groaned. "I hate waiting. I'm really hoping he sent you some family pictures. I want to see what Mum looks like when she's old."

"I don't need Billy's package to tell you that," I answered, twisting again to look for Matt. "You only have to see your Gran. I'd bet money on that."

"What odds?" she laughed and then sobered. "Seriously, Thad, look after yourself. Everyone here knows about the bets, and that Jonesy and his mob had to ask their fathers to help. People are laughing at them, saying they deserved it. That won't make him happy. Be careful."

"Matt says he probably won't try anything until they've paid everyone off." From the corner of my eye I saw Matt beckoning and finished, "Gotta go."

Chaplain Thomas opened his house for lunch every Wednesday. Thanks to Chloe's call and my lack of mobility, Matt and I arrived last. Surprisingly, the room was full. A boy from my English class offered his chair, and Matt found a place on the floor nearby. I didn't know any of the songs they sang, but Chaplain Thomas's talk was funny. Basically, I enjoyed the hour.

"I'm surprised so many were there," I told Matt as they walked back towards the classrooms.

"Good food. That's probably why half of them come."

With the addition of lunch with Chaplain Thomas, my schedule was set. Rowing before school, math tutoring, my special Greek seminars on Tuesday and Thursday mornings, and then, afternoon school. Afterwards, physio and weight training. Then, dinner, homework, free time and bed.

Sometimes, I walked to the cricket ovals to watch Matt practicing. Plus, I made good use of my library card. Saturdays came as a complete surprise. King William's had a policy that everyone played for or represented the school. Only illness or something like that excused us from debating, or playing chess and playing various sports. After we competed, we had to cheer for our fellow Dubbees in their matches. I went with the rowing teams if a regatta were held. Otherwise, I watched Matt's team. King William's turned out to be even more structured than my convict life. The twenty-first century wasn't chaos, after all.

It took three weeks, but I was finally able to meet the archivist. As she handed Billy's gift to me her eyes were full of questions, but she showed me to a private room and gave me gloves to handle the papers, saying, "No matter how careful you are, you will contaminate old paper if you don't wear them."

I waited till she'd grudgingly left the room before I untied the brown paper wrapping. Inside was a beautiful box. "Oh, Billy," I said quietly. Somehow, the box with its embossed leather and marbled cardboard made more of a distance between Billy and me than there had ever been. The Billy I'd known would put a frog in the box to startle me. This Billy, the one who appreciated beauty, I wished I'd known.

The box was capacious. It needed to be, for Billy had crammed it full of letters and photos. I glanced through these, hoping to find one for Chloe and her father. The best was a group portrait. Lord and Lady Peter sat on Wahmurra's front verandah on chairs from their library. Billy and a woman I thought must be Polly stood behind them, next to their spouses. Children sat in front of their parents and grandparents.

The number surprised me. I would have expected at least ten, but there were only five. Billy, it seemed, had three sons; Polly, two daughters. Why didn't they or their descendants own Wahmurra? What had happened? Some financial disaster? A medical one?

I had just begun to sort through the papers when the bell rang. I put everything away, except for a diary and the group photograph. When I started to leave, however, the archivist stopped me. "What are you doing? You can't borrow those!"

"I'm not borrowing. I'm taking. Billy Kendricks left these for me, and I want to show them to a friend."

"They're part of the Kendricks Special Collection," the archivist said, and from the look on her face, she knew she'd rather die than let a piece of paper, much less a photograph, leave the building.

"Billy left them for me. They're my property."

"Sir William," she corrected, looking at me as though I were snail's slime.

I knew which battles to fight. "Sir William left the box for me."

She smiled as though she'd won the war. "The exact words in the bequest, I believe, are 'To be opened only by Thaddeus Compton.' You have to leave everything here. You can come back and see it any time the archives are open, but you cannot take anything out of here."

I didn't know whether to laugh or cry. Chloe didn't have any problem figuring out how she felt. She was mad. "Can't you do anything? Ask Mr. White to make her give them to you?"

"That would be bullying. Besides, where would I keep them? There's another letter in code, so I'll ask if you can help me with it next Friday. You could get a taxi over here. Then your dad can pick us up when the archives close, or we'll take my train down to Sydney."

Although separated by only a few miles, our schools were on different railway lines. Both lines started in Sydney and ended in Hornsby, but they took different routes to get there. Chloe's went over the Harbour Bridge. Mine wended its way through inner city suburbs before crossing the Parramatta River and heading north. Students at Enderby and King William's were always cadging rides back and forth between the schools. What might take up to three-quarters of an hour by train, depending on connections, took ten minutes by car or taxi.

"We have to go by train anyway. Dad will be back in the States, and Gran's just got back from her cruise," Chloe answered.

I stretched out in my armchair and held the phone closer. "Chloe, do you think I could ask Matt for the weekend? He usually doesn't go anywhere, even when we're allowed to leave school." I shifted his phone to my other ear and looked across the room to Matt's family photos, "His mum's battling to keep their property, after the drought nearly wiped them out, and he's a great friend. What do you think?"

"I think Gran will love having another male to spoil, and I bet she'll fall in love with his smile."

I wanted to say, *"Just make sure you don't,"* but I stopped myself. I couldn't fall in love. Neither of us knew where I'd end up. In any case, I was too young. Wasn't I?

14

While waiting for Visiting Friday, I studied Billy's letters whenever I could get to the archives. After a while I figured out that Billy was telling me only one thing: there were more gates between his world and the twenty-first century one besides the yellow brick. I kept wondering what Billy knew that had made him so desperate to get that knowledge to me. Why did he think I'd need it? When would I need it?

I didn't mind worrying about these questions, but Jonesy, Beresford and their friends did their best to make my life miserable. Things went missing or turned up in the most humiliating places. Just before she'd left, Gran had given me $100 and told me to spend it on something fun. When I saw a pair of vivid shoes on special, I rushed in and bought them.

I don't know why I loved them, but I wore them whenever I could. One morning though, they were found on the hat peg in the teachers' common room, and I was given three detentions for disrespect. On the last day of the cricket season, someone covered the "Thaddeus Compton Oval" signboard. When Matt and I walked under it to get seats for the senior match, someone pulled a string and everyone laughed when they saw the sign altered to read "MY OVAL."

Most of King William's students joined the school's

cadet corps. It was another tradition, one that had begun way back in the nineteenth century. According to the corps' recruiting poster, it aimed to teach discipline and leadership in addition to military skills. When I'd seen the squads drilling from my room in the infirmary, I thought I'd enjoy being a cadet.

There was one obstacle. Jonesy's squad was short on numbers and would be broken up if it couldn't enlist new members. I became the obvious target. Mr. Graham tried first and looked disappointed when I refused. "It's not because I don't want to be a cadet. I do," I told Matt later. "I just don't want to be part of anything Jonesy runs. Can't you enlist me in yours?"

Matt shook his head. His squad was full to overflowing. A couple of days later, Jonesy himself tried to change my mind. "You'll like it. It's great fun," he told me. I thought he had to be the biggest fool on earth if he thought I'd believe him.

I didn't even bother looking him in the face. I just mumbled, "No, thanks," and walked away.

"The problem is I don't trust him. I don't understand why Mr. Graham thinks he's such a good leader. He's nothing but a bully," I told Matt later.

To my total surprise, Matt looked worried. "He's got a good reputation in the corps," he answered slowly. "I think that's his element. Everything is clear cut. Nothing's gray. I think Jonesy flourishes when things are black and white. But, you'll have a bigger problem if you don't join the cadets. What will you do during camps week?"

I groaned. "Don't tell me. Another tradition? What's camps week anyway?"

Matt pulled his army boots out and began polishing them for inspection the next day. "For cadets," he said after he'd studied one boot for spots, "It's the week when we go into the bush. We set up camp, do army stuff, like shoot at targets. We're sent on missions with only regular army food, dried meat. That kind of stuff." He gave his boots a final flick with the polishing cloth. "Hey, while I've got the polish out, want your shoes done?"

"Of course. Why bother asking?" I tossed my shoes across the room and watched while Matt brushed the black polish onto them. "Matt? What happens to the guys who aren't cadets during camps week? What do we do?"

"Community service."

"What's that?"

All kinds of things, according to Matt. I might be sent to help with meals on wheels, or graffiti removal. Or, I might find myself reading to children in inner city libraries. But the more I thought about it and imagined the fun I could have in the bush, joining cadets became a no-brainer. I'd be back in my element in the bush, and I knew I could handle Jonesy, Beresford, and friends. Not only handle them, but give them a taste of their own medicine. As I thought about the possibilities, I couldn't stop smiling. Jonesy would have a huge surprise coming.

I went to Mr. Graham, signed the enlistment papers, got kitted out, and began drilling with the squad. When Jonesy gave me the parental consent form for camp, I couriered it off to Mr. White.

Dr. Rivers sent for me in the middle of my last class the following afternoon. "I've canceled you out of camp," he announced. "Dr. Mansfield was very hesitant about it, so Mr. White refused to give consent."

As my happiness vanished, I knew what a deflated balloon felt like and just how much I'd been looking forward to a week in the bush. "What will I do instead? Paint over graffiti?"

"Not even that, I'm afraid. Dr. Mansfield refused that as

well. Actually he preferred camp to it. He's still not convinced that your immune system is completely healthy. He suggested you do something around here."

I looked around Dr. Rivers' gleaming office with its models of antique cars. One wall showcased various woods, like cedars and eucalypti. For the first time King William's resembled a gilded cage. "Around here? Around King William's? What would I do?"

Dr. Rivers moved his shoulders in a gesture that would have been called a shrug if I'd done it. "Thad, there's a bottom line here. Mr. White will not let you attend cadet camp, and he's threatened to hire security guards if you do inner city community work. I suppose he has his reasons."

When I looked at him, I realized Dr. Rivers felt as frustrated as I did. Both of us knew most Dubbees wouldn't understand and might think I'd bought my way out of camps or something weird like that. "What about Mr. Murray? If he faxed permission, would that do it?"

Dr. Rivers looked to me. "Do you seriously expect me to tell Mr. White that I went over his head?"

I shook my head. "Last ditch hope, sir."

Dr. Rivers actually sighed. "Anyway, the question's moot. You can't go, even if Mr. Murray signs you off, because Dr. Mansfield won't sign your medical certificate. It's as simple as that and that means, because of your medical exemption, you have a free week. Rather than mope around here by yourself, I suggest you go to Wahmurra. There's only a half day after camps before the term ends, and I can excuse you from that."

"Sir," I began, but Dr. Rivers cut me off.

I got the impression that he'd already told Mr. White everything I wanted to say and was thoroughly fed up with both me and camps week. "I'm sorry, Thad. Unless you can think of some way to change Dr. Mansfield's mind, the decision's made. Hopefully, things will be easier next year. Now, tell me about your rowing. I understand Coach is very pleased with you."

I didn't want to talk about rowing, but I kept my cool and politely answered Dr. Rivers' questions before being excused. For once, I didn't want to go to the archives. Instead, I went to my room and threw myself onto the bed. I was still steaming mad when Matt walked in.

"I feel like I'm a baby or something," I stormed. "I know I could have ambushed Jonesy in the bush and paid him back. Now, he'll despise me worse than ever. I'm the only boy in the entire school that's not allowed to go to camp. Even if I did, Mr. White said he'd hire security guards. I hate security guards."

"Thad, come on. Don't be a drama queen. Everyone as rich as you has security with them. In most cases, all the time."

I pulled out a pair of jeans and began to change for dinner. "I'm not rich-rich, not like Jason Billingsley."

"No, you're not. You have an extra 0 or two on everything Jason has in his bank account," Matt retorted.

My cheeks went red. I really hadn't thought much about money since the time I'd been too poor to buy bread for my family back in London. "I'm not like Billingsley, and you know it."

Jason Billingsley continually boasted of his father's wealth. His clothes, as he often pointed out, hadn't been bought in the school store. They were tailored. He mentioned this and the size of his family's yacht frequently. A stretch limousine delivered him to school each day, and now I realized that the man who opened the limo's door must double as a bodyguard.

"No, you're not Billingsley," Matt agreed. "You're in a different league, although you don't seem to know it. You're the Compton Trust. Nobody can top that—not in Australia. If you don't think you're different though, look around you. I've been here since I was ten, but I've only visited Dr. Rivers' office once—the day I arrived."

"So?"

"So, you've been there three times in four weeks that I know about. Of course," he went on, pushing his hair back in a typical Matt gesture, "the real difference is that you're paying for me to be here. I'm a Compton Scholar. My mother can't afford King William's, so the school gave me one of your scholarships." His voice faded to nothing, and he turned his face away from me as though he thought it would make a difference.

I didn't know what to say. I put my yellow shoes on slowly. I wished I could tell him the truth. Instead, as we left for dinner, I put an arm over his shoulder, "I've already talked this over with Chloe and her grandmother. How about coming to Double Bay with me for the weekend?"

It didn't take long for my camps exemption to become common knowledge. One afternoon after classes, Jonesy and Beresford cornered me. "You're nothing but bleeding geekpoop, Compton," Jonesy sneered. "I don't care how many ovals or boats are named after you. To me, and every decent Dubbee, you're geekpoop, a mommy's boy."

"No," Beresford chimed in, "he's Whitey's boy. Without Mr. White behind you, you're dirt, Compton. In fact, you …" he broke off and blushed furiously when his voice broke.

"You should go around in bubble wrap seeing you're so-oo fragile," Jonesy finished.

Not hauling off and smashing Jonesy's face to pulp was the hardest thing I'd ever done. As the days passed, I regretted my promise not to fight even more. A white rose mysteriously appeared on my desk every English class.

When I wouldn't explain its significance, I, not Jonesy, got a detention. Matt suspected that a day boy brought the rose into school, but we couldn't figure out who.

Worse was the ostracism. When I walked into rooms, conversation stopped, and everyone became as silent of mute swans. Of course, it wasn't the majority in my class or even School House. But it was obvious, and it annoyed the stuffing out of me.

Visiting Friday couldn't come fast enough. I haunted the archives, and by the time Chloe arrived, I'd read almost everything Billy had left. Mrs. Christie more than approved of this diligence. "When you're assigned your history project next term," she told me with a smile, "you should do it on Sir William. He was one of our earliest students and maybe the school's greatest benefactor. You'll find lots of material here and at the State Archives."

When I told Chloe this, she nodded her head. "We have to do one too. Maybe I'll do mine on Polly, and we can share the work. Now, show me the photographs."

As we turned towards the road leading to King William's archives, something became obvious. I stopped and stood still. "You've had your hair cut," I grumbled.

"I'm training for swimming again. What is it with males and long hair? I don't get it."

While she looked through Billy's photos, I thought about her long hair, streaming behind her like a golden, elongated halo, as she jumped to catch the cat-o-nine-tails whip used in my flogging. I'd never forget it; it was etched into my memory. I left her with the photos, and went over to School House to collect Matt and finish packing.

My backpack was stuffed by the time I finished. Because camps week was the last week of Term 1, I packed my winter traveling outfit as well as everything else. "Hurry up, Thad," Matt called out from the front door. "You'll be back here in three weeks."

"In a minute. I can't find one of my shoes." I'd looked forward to showing the yellow shoes to Gran ever since I'd bought them.

I'd worried that having Matt around would destroy my happiness at Gran's, but Matt proved an ideal guest. I'd secretly arranged with Mrs. Christie to have the Kendricks daguerreotype copied and framed, and when I gave it to Gran, she was overwhelmed. She stared at Lady Peter's face, at the daughter she'd lost through time, and tears ran unchecked down her face. Then, seemingly without realizing it, she dropped her own bombshell.

"That's Eliza, my great-grandmother," she announced, pointing to Polly's eldest daughter. "She lived to be nearly ninety. I can still remember visiting her."

When I looked at Chloe, she seemed shocked but completely happy. "Do you mean Polly is my great-something grandmother?"

"Of course. This house is willed through to the daughters of the family. Didn't you know?" Gran's voice was placid and I wondered if she really didn't know the effect her words had on Chloe.

"But I didn't know I was related to *Polly*," Chloe retorted. "Why didn't you say something? You know I met her."

Gran shut her mouth like the proverbial steep trap, and even Matt knew there was a mystery she wouldn't divulge until she was good and ready. But without knowing it, she'd answered one of my questions. Though the Kendricks might have lost Wahmurra, they hadn't lost the Double Bay house. Polly must have inherited it.

In a rare gesture of trust, Mr. White had told me to take the train as far north as Broadmeadow, by myself, *sans* security guards or anyone else. On Sunday, when the three of us set off from Double Bay, the plan was that Matt would get off the train with Chloe at her station and taxi across to King William's. I'd continue on to Hornsby and then change to the North Coast XPT.

Just before we left, Gran produced a small rolling bag. "There are work boots, warm socks, wool shirts and sweaters in here," she told me. "Mr. White asked for them. And here's spending money for the train," she added, handing fifty dollars to each of us. When Matt refused to take it, she gave him her best Gran-stare, "You're a part of the family now, Matt. You cleaned up the kitchen when I asked, so why should I treat you differently? Enjoy the money, and don't forget I'm expecting you the first Visiting Friday in Term 2."

As the train rolled out of the Wynyard train station and we settled in for the ride, Matt looked over to Chloe. "Look, about Visiting Fridays. I don't know what Enderby's like, but Term 2 for us is the horrors. We go to dances all the time."

"I know. We're always hosting them," Chloe nodded.

I stopped poking around in the bag of food Gran had sent and looked at them. "What are you two talking about?"

Chloe face was horrified. "I've just realized. You can't dance, can you?"

"If you call hopping up and down like you do dancing, then I can't," Thad told her. "I can waltz though. What's so funny?" I asked when they burst out laughing.

Matt stopped first. "Thad, nobody waltzes anymore. Not at our age, anyway. But the real reason we're laughing is that all the girls' schools, like Enderby, hold dances nearly every weekend in Term 2. It's the schools' way of making sure no one gets into trouble, and it's supposed to give us boarders something to look forward to. But they're dreadful things. We have to wear our good pants and blazers."

I pulled a face, but I didn't really care. I'd basically lost control of choosing my own clothes the moment the policeman grabbed me back in London. For Matt, it seemed a tragedy.

"At least the girls wear pretty dresses. Not that you can look at them," he continued sounding glum. "There's always teachers and house parents going around making sure you get up and dance all the time. Plus, they serve warm punch. The food's inedible. Even if we go to Enderby, and Enderby's food's okay, Chloe, but even at Enderby, you'd only be able to dance with Chloe once. Twice, if you're lucky. The whole idea is that we socialize. It's all right for some, but I hate Term 2 Fridays with a passion."

It sounded dreadful and, for a moment, I thought that Chloe might say that Matt was wrong. She loved dancing and was always gyrating around at Gran's with earphones in her ears. But she nodded moodily, "He's right, Thad. Friday nights are usually awful. We have to dance with whoever asks us. That's why I know and loathe Bruce Jones. He's a groper."

As she and Matt told horror stories to each other, I wondered if my medical exemption could be extended to school dances. Probably not. No way I could get so lucky. I stared out the window at the passing scenery and only got galvanized when the train left Pymble, and Chloe began her best Gran imitation. "Thad, you know you have to change platforms at Hornsby, don't you?" she began, and I fully expected her to tell me not to talk to strangers.

Then it was time for hurried good-byes. I'd see her in two weeks, when Gran brought her up to Wahmurra. It would be three weeks before I saw Matt again and the dreaded dance term began.

On the train to Broadmeadow, I began to think I could function in Chloe's world. No one looked at me strangely, I managed to buy my dinner without drawing attention to myself, and I enjoyed looking out the window until it got dark. Best of all, I saw Jim, Mr. White's driver, as soon as I left the train.

"Take your time, young Thad," Jim told me. "The boss said to take everything slowly. There's a bit of trouble, I'm afraid."

15

Jim said he'd leave it to Mr. White to tell about the "bit of trouble," so I fretted the entire way to Wahmurra, and there wasn't the sense of peace or homecoming I'd felt in January. When Jim told me to hide my face when we drove past the Barracks, I was thoroughly spooked.

Once they reached the House, Mr. White gave me his equivalent to a hug, and I felt marginally better. Then he told me to put my things in Billy's room and meet him in the library.

Once there, I used every bit of patience I possessed as he poured me a cup of tea and then produced a brandy snifter and his cut-glass bottle of cognac. I fidgeted while he swirled the brandy in the snifter, and then my patience snapped. "Please tell me, Mr. White. What's the matter? Jim said there was trouble."

"Possible trouble," Mr. White amended and continued to contemplate his cognac.

"What possible trouble?"

"Frank Bundy's here."

Of all the possible situations I'd imagined, Frank Bundy hadn't made the list. I'd believed Wahmurra was Bundy-proof, that Mr. White would protect me against his prying eyes. I couldn't imagine any scenario in which Mr. White allowed Frank Bundy to stay alive while on Wahmurra land.

I slumped back against the armchair, wishing I were older and could asked Mr. White to pour me a gallon of cognac. Tea just didn't cut it. "How's that possible?" I stammered eventually.

"Majestic Television booked a retreat for its senior executives months ago, and we worked with them to set up some 'bonding' scenarios. I checked the list of executives myself. Mr. Bundy's name was not on the original list, I assure you. If it had been," Mr. White said in his deceptively fragile voice, "I would have canceled."

"But... But he came anyway?" I asked, twisting one foot into Mr. White's prized Persian rug. I might gouge a hole in it but I didn't care. I wanted to feel poised to run away at any moment if Bundy appeared.

"Apparently he was a last minute replacement," Mr. White answered, making a moue of distaste with his mouth. "I phoned Majestic's president immediately and told him that if Mr. Bundy went as much as one millimeter out of bounds, or if he came more than fifty meters near this house, I'd send the whole lot packing without a refund. I even threatened financial repercussions if his prized investigative reporter misbehaved. He gave me his word."

Suddenly, I felt the need for sweet hot tea. After I finished the cupful, I leaned forward. "Do you believe he'll behave himself?"

Mr. White laughed. It seemed incongruous, but when he began speaking again, he reminded me of the other Mr. White, the one I'd known back in 1833. No one trifled with that Mr. White. I looked across at this Mr. White's face in the firelight and knew that the president of Majestic Television would do everything he could to keep Frank Bundy in line.

But that brought up another question. "Will he be able to? I mean, will Frank Bundy listen to his president and do what he's told?"

When Mr. White swirled his cognac again, my eyes followed the liquid round and round the snifter. "Mr. Bundy's extremely good at what he does. However, times are tough, and good jobs are scarce," he replied eventually. "Everyone's on full alert. It means your week has changed, though. I'd originally arranged for you to help some pensioners down in Barrington. That's too close now. Instead, and with Dr. Rivers' approval, I've offered you to a social services agency across the bay. You'll take the power boat. It's too far to row. Jim will teach you how to use it tomorrow. I'm afraid it's back to convict hours for a week. Up at the crack of dawn, and home again at dark. If we're careful, no one will see you. I think this is better than surrounding you with guards."

Mr. White's idea sounded good—in theory at least.

As the week flew by, I relaxed and felt more and more confident and forgot about Frank Bundy's exceptional curiosity. When I powered back to Wahmurra on Thursday night, I was knackered. I'd chopped and stacked firewood for some seniors all day. My shoulders ached. I yearned for a hot bath. Back at Wahmurra, I scrambled out of the boat nimbly enough, only to stop dead in my tracks when a voice hailed me.

"Hey, there." it said and, even though I'd never heard Frank Bundy's voice, I knew who it was immediately.

"I need help," he went on, watching as I secured the boat. "I have to get to Too Far Island tomorrow without being seen. It's our last challenge, and if I can do it, I'll win the competition. It looks impossible, but I thought someone who lived around here might know a way to do it. I'd be very grateful, believe me."

I shivered, grateful for the cold breeze that allowed me to pull my collar up and my hat down, while I stared out at the island. "If I were you, sir," I answered slowly, making sure my mid-Pacific vowels were firmly in place, "I'd hide a rowboat somewhere behind the point over there behind Oyster Creek. Then, tomorrow, when you're told to start, all you have to do is walk down the track, get the boat and row. Everyone will be watching the marina, so you can't take a power boat. It would be missed. But no one will count the rowboats. That's your best bet. Row to the far side down there, and you'll be invisible from here." *And, it's as far from the House as you can get.*

"Will you take me now and show me? We could tow the rowboat and leave it there. I'll give you fifty bucks."

I stamped my feet. My toes were cold, and I wished I'd worn two pairs of Gran's woolen socks. "I suppose so, if you don't think it's cheating," I answered, before getting a dinghy and looping its rope round a stanchion on the power boat. "When you're ready, sir."

As we made our way past Oyster Creek, Bundy leaned back. "It's funny how life turns out, isn't it?" he began conversationally. "One of my ancestors was a convict here doing who knows what. Now, nearly two hundred years later, my boss pays five thousand a day for me to be here. Twenty-five thousand for five days. I don't think my great-great-great grandfather ever imagined there was that much money in the entire world, or had five thousand in his life. Yet, here I am, living the life of Reilly, walking on ground he must have walked on. I tell you, it gives me the shivers when I think about it."

I suddenly understood why Frank Bundy was so good at his job. People wanted to divulge their biggest secrets to him. I wanted to tell him all about Ol' Bundy and what he was really like. It took a real effort to keep my lips sealed, but I listened carefully as Frank went on in his persuasive voice, "Coming here has made me realize how lucky I am to live in this century. My ancestor probably never had a chance in England. Maybe, he was just a boy when he came out here as a convict with no hope of a future."

No, I was the young boy with no future, I wanted to shout and was grateful when a wave rocked the boat and made me concentrate on getting Frank and the rowboat to their destination as quickly as possible and before I might succumb to the temptation to talk about Ol' Bundy. I could hardly wait to race back to the House and repeat the whole conversation to Mr. White. I wanted his opinion. Was it possible that Frank Bundy had somehow found out about me and spun the whole sob story to see how I reacted? If so, who had talked?

At dinner, Mr. White listened attentively. I finished by saying, "I wanted to tell him what the old so-and-so was really like. Then I started wondering if that was his way of getting me to talk. He seemed so genuine."

Mr. White's face hardened, and his eyes were laser sharp as they studied me. "Are you positive that you didn't let anything slip?"

"Once I understood that I was tempted to, I was too scared to say much except point out the way back to the Barracks. I tell you, Mr. White. I had the boat at full throttle on the way back. Then, I came up to the House by the back way. You know, up the cliff overlooking Lady's Cove. I made sure he couldn't see me."

Mr. White put the last morsel of sole into his mouth and pushed his plate away. "Thad, the number of people who know everything about you is exactly five—me, Chloe, her dad, Gran, and Dr. Mansfield. That's all. Do you imagine any of us letting your secret out?"

I shook my head. "No, but sir, when I was in Greenway, I swear it was Ol' Bundy I saw, not Frank. Their hair is the same color, but their faces are different. It's been worrying me ever since, because I've wondered if he could have found a way through to this time. It can't only be me and Chloe, Billy and maybe Polly who can go back and forth. Maybe Ol' Bundy's got here, and he can't go back either. Maybe he found Frank Bundy and he's telling him everything."

Mr. White studied me for several moments. "I don't think you're right about that, Thad," he said eventually. "I don't understand the going back and forth, as you call it. Don't forget that half of the time you were in Greenway, you seemed out of your mind. Maybe, we've underestimated Mr. Bundy. Maybe, we're reading too much into innocent talk. He could be as genuine about finding out about his ancestor as he sounds. I'll certainly look into it. That's one thing you can be sure of."

When Mr. White left the room to have his port and read in the library, I usually went to see what was on television. Thanks to Wahmurra's communications set-up, there was always something I was interested in. But tonight I went back for a novel I was reading and rejoined Mr. White in the library. When we said goodnight though, something popped into my mind, and without thinking, I asked, "Mr. White, did you ever find a gate between the worlds and go back yourself?"

16

Mr. White didn't answer, and I wondered if he'd heard. As the days went by I was too intimidated to ask it again, but I couldn't stop thinking about the possibility. Maybe time travel explained why Mr. White had the Midas touch with investments—with his own, and those of the Compton Trust. That explained how he knew what to invest in.

When Chloe arrived a week later, I dragged her immediately down to Lady's Cove and told her about my conversation with Frank Bundy and then the unanswered question I'd asked Mr. White. To my surprise, she merely looked thoughtful and didn't answer immediately.

The next day we rode out to a densely forested gorge. There didn't appear to be any place for the horses to graze, much less for us to have a picnic. But once we wriggled through a gap in the trees, a creek crashed and splashed its way down the hill, racing towards Wahmurra Bay, and tree ferns outlined a grassy space where I set out our picnic.

"You know," Chloe said while she hobbled the horses, "I've been thinking if anyone from 1833 went around hunting for time-gates, it would be the 1833 version of Mr. White. Plus, there's something funny about this Mr. White. Gran won't talk about him, and it took me every bit of persuasion I possess to make her come up here with me."

"She seems to be enjoying herself," Thad said as he piled food onto his plate. The House cooks had always packed great lunches, and this meal was no different. Meat pies, sandwiches, a mango salad, and lots of fruit.

"Yes, she does," Chloe conceded, "but only after she got the trip down to the convict church out of the way. It broke my heart when I showed her the pew Mom must have disappeared from. I think Gran was scared that if she touched it, she'd go back to 1833 as well."

"Maybe she wanted to," Thad answered.

"I don't think so. But something certainly happened between her and Mr. White in the past. She's never talked about it, and I don't see her changing her mind now."

I threw a couple of crusts to a pair of fairy wrens, but a hungry rosella chased them away. After scattering more crusts, I turned back to Chloe. "But, Mr. White likes her. You can tell. I wonder what happened."

Another mystery. Another Mr. White mystery. There were far too many for my liking.

All too soon, it was time for Term 2. It felt strange dressing in King William's winter uniform of long pants and long sleeved shirt, but even stranger because I still had to wear the stupid boater. Chloe's hat changed with the seasons, because she now wore a dark green one with the Enderby green and gold striped hatband. Twenty-first century schools had the weirdest rules.

As soon as Gran dropped me off, I got right back into King William's activities. Training became crucial as Coach prepped Jonesy and me for the big Cook's River race. Thousands had signed up, so the race committee ran elimination rounds every day for a week to weed the numbers down. Jonesy would race on the first Saturday, but I drew the worst possible slot—the very last race a week later. The twenty fastest times would make the final.

"What's the big deal about the race?" Chloe wanted to know one day after school. "Rowing's supposed to be over."

"That's why the race is happening now. Some guy saw a schoolboys' race in London and put up money for this one. But because he'd never gone to a school with a rowing team, he opened it up to anyone. I don't think anyone thought there'd be so much interest."

"Huge money. That will favor schools with rowing teams."

I shook my head. "No. We have to row in ordinary dinghies against the incoming tide, and anyone between twelve and fifteen can have a go at it. "

"Not anyone," Chloe commented immediately. "It's males only."

"Only for this year." I couldn't work out the twenty-first century's insistence on gender equality. For me, it always came down to one thing. Only females could have babies. Ergo, gender difference, but I'd learned enough to keep those thoughts in my head. "Coach doesn't quite know what to make of the whole thing. They're sending us off in batches every fifteen minutes. There'll be lots of stragglers."

"You'll do fine, Thad. It's your kind of race."

"I'll do my best. Gotta go. There's the homework bell." As I walked towards School House, I wondered if she'd be right, and that I would have a real chance. My leg was almost back to full strength and the days of needing crutches were a distance memory.

Jonesy had trouble adjusting to the race. When we arrived for his race, he could not have shown his contempt more obviously. Then, to Coach's horror, and in typical Jonesy manner, he sprinted out front. He would have won if the race had been a mere half mile. However, he had two more miles to go. He finished a distant second and had to wait until the very end, my race, to find out if he qualified.

And, as usual, he was totally unrepentant. "Stupid, stupid race," he scoffed, as he sat under a tree and threw twigs and leaves around. "Ninety percent of them hadn't been in a boat before. They shouldn't have been allowed to compete."

Training sessions now became even more of an endurance challenge as Jonesy tried to blame me for his own performance. His friends slapped wet towels against me if the seniors weren't around, and shouldered me into the lockers more times than I could count. Given this animosity, I fully expected that Jonesy would find some excuse not to watch my race, but he surprised me by turning out with the rest of the club.

Because my race was the very last one, the tactics were easy. I simply had to row flat out with zero margin for error. "Don't mess around out there, Thad," Coach told me. "Jones did, and it looks like he won't get through to the final. King William's needs you. Don't play around out there."

I did have a plan and, fortunately, Coach agreed with it. We'd studied the river, and the way it meandered towards Botany Bay. Jonesy had proved that straight line rowing was useless. I planned to row steadily for the first mile, then navigate my way through any stragglers from the previous heats before sprinting for the finish.

There were at least five experienced rowers in my race. That is, if skintight suits meant experience. That made things easier. They would set a good pace and, as long as I kept them behind me, I'd have a chance for a fast time. I didn't think they'd worry about me because I wore a tee-shirt and rugby shorts. No skintights for me.

When the starter's gun went, they set off in a bunch, and I happily trailed them. They managed to keep together until we reached the first of the stragglers. After we passed the bridge at Tempe, I shot past them and lost myself amongst even more stragglers. I maneuvered through them and was increasing my speed when I passed the finish line.

Somewhat astonished that the end had come so quickly, I rowed across to the officials' tent and checked in. Coach was ecstatic. I'd got the best overall time. When we raced for real the following Saturday, I'd start as the top seed in the center of the river.

After I'd toweled down, we had to hang around until it became obvious that Jonesy had just squeaked into the final with the nineteenth best time. He'd start far to my right on the outside bank and hopefully stay out of my way.

I quickly found out there was one huge disadvantage to owning the fastest qualifying time. Majestic TV had bought the right to televise the race and wanted to interview me. At first I was fine with it. Then I discovered the interviewer's identity--Frank Bundy.

"I can't do it, Coach. Ask Jonesy. He'll do a much better job."

"They want you, Thad. You're the one with the fastest time."

I pulled my rowing cap down over my eyebrows. "Sir, I'll be a disaster. Jonesy would love it. I'll only do it if Dr. Rivers tells me I have to."

As Coach stumped his way over to Jonesy, I thought I'd hear about my refusal more than once in the next few days, but the interview Jonesy gave was good. More than good, it was brilliant and the cameras loved him. They emphasized his handsomeness and, as he smiled the entire time, he came across as a humble, good looking kid with a horrible starting position. "I expect to be beaten," he finished while smiling at Frank Bundy. "But, I also expect to do my best and bring honor to King William's and my rowing club."

When the interview aired later that night, School House's junior common room erupted into jeers. "You don't expect to win?" someone shouted at Jonesy. "Yesterday you told me that if you had money to spare, you'd give fifty to one that you'll beat Thad."

"Bring honor to King William's and the rowing club?" another taunted. "Since when do you know what honor means?"

Jonesy's friends stood up and wanted to take the fight outside, but Jonesy was in too good a mood. "I did a good job, didn't I?" he smiled. "Did anyone record it?"

Coach thanked him the next morning and then devoted the rest of the week to fine tuning our rowing. Jonesy seemed to bask in everyone's praise, so I was surprised when the first wet towel slapped me in the locker room on Friday, the day before the race. Cursing myself for letting my guard down, I faced Jonesy who was flanked, as usual, by Kyle Beresford, Andrew Alton and a couple of other friends.

"That got your attention, didn't it, Whitey's-boy?" Jonesy began, and from the look on his face I knew something worse was to happen. "Pity we can't leave a mark on you," he went on. "But you'd only show it to Coach, wouldn't you?"

"Maybe he'd cry on his phone to Chloe Murray," Kyle suggested.

I'll kill him if he brings Chloe into this.

The normally rowdy room had gone dead silent. Half the rowers crowded the section where I was, while others drifted into the showers or sat in front of their lockers. I wondered if any of them would be like Matt and stand my friend.

"He'll have to do something to keep her interested. Everyone knows she's got the attention span of a butterfly," Andrew Alton told Jonesy.

I wondered if he'd ever met Chloe.

"Kyle's our expert on Miss Chloe," Jonesy went on. "Why, it was only this past Christmas she slept with him.

Only lasted a week though. What was the matter, Kyle? You or her?"

"Boring. She was so-ooo boring. The sweetness thing only went so..." He broke off as my fist crashed into his jaw and he dropped to the floor.

"You're lying," I shouted, standing over him. "You never met her over Christmas, I know that. Now, admit it, or I'll kill you."

"Now there's a threat—but only if you believe Whitey's boy has some backbone," Jonesy drawled as Andrew hauled Kyle to his feet. "You want me, Whitey's boy, don't you? Well, come on. I know you're jealous, because I'm the one they chose for the TV interview. Let's have that fight we've been talking about for weeks, or don't you have the guts?"

When I looked around the room, a dozen rowers in various stages of undress stared back at me. I glared at Jonesy. I knew he'd manipulated me into this fight and that it was wrong. But I also knew I'd never forgive myself if I didn't defend Chloe. I looked at Jonesy and there was raw rage in my voice when I said, "If this is the only way to shut your mouth up about Chloe, then I hope you're ready to apologize. You can do it now—or later if your jaw is still working. No matter, I want an apology."

For a second Jonesy stared at me, and I thought he might actually apologize. Out of the corner of his eye I noticed a couple of boys leave the room. I didn't blame them. I wouldn't want to watch a massacre.

Jonesy threw the wet towel in his hands into a nearby bin and advanced. "Well, well," he said with a smile. "Right, and now we'll see what Whitey's boy is really made of."

He didn't have time to say more. I'd learnt to fight from watching convicts. They'd never waited till someone rang a starting bell so, before he expected anything, I exploded into action, throwing myself against him and pushing him hard against the lockers. Once I'd pinned him there, I punched his face and jabbed into his ribs.

Jonesy seemed bewildered by the rapidity of my attack. He tried pushing me away, but I just continued pounding his rib cage. The hollering that began in the room with the first punch died away. Jonesy landed a couple of good hits to my head, but he couldn't stop me. He hadn't been a convict, and he'd learned fighting from teachers, not the real world. When he staggered, I switched tactics and sent uppercuts towards his jaw, looking for the knockout punch.

No one noticed when the door opened, or when Coach, Luke and some other seniors rushed into the room. After they pried us apart, Coach exploded when he saw our bloodied faces and shouted, "Have you two forgotten you're supposed to row three and a half miles tomorrow? What on earth are you two doing?"

"Having a boxing exhibition, sir," I panted, fighting the hammerlock Luke had on me.

Jonesy knew the code as well. "Just a bit of fun, sir."

"Pre-race nerves, Coach," one of the spectators contributed.

"Pre-race nerves my eye," Coach muttered. "I'll deal with you two on Monday, after the race. The race that's tomorrow, in case you haven't remembered. The race one of you is expected to win. Now, get your clothes on and get into the bus. Luke, you stay with Compton, Peter, you're with Jones. I don't want them sitting near each other or even talking. Understood?"

As we obediently trooped away, Coach fired one last salvo, "Jones, you stay away from the television cameras, understand? I'm not having the whole world seeing your black and blue face. And get some steak to put on that eye."

17

The next day I listened while Coach told Jonesy and me that we must conserve energy and take the first part of the race easy. I knew I couldn't row that way. In a normal regatta, where every rower has his own lane, it might work. But this race? Twenty dinghies would fight over the same narrow space. I planned to sprint the first seven hundred yards or so, evaluate, and do whatever it took to stay in front of everyone else.

The majority of rowers must have heard similar advice to Coach's, because they started conservatively. But two rowers challenged me immediately—a burly kid in ordinary shorts and a singlet, and Jonesy, who sprinted across to the middle after the gun sounded. I knew then that he had his own strategy and wasn't paying attention to Coach either. He'd decided that I was his main opposition, for he shadowed every move I made. If I sped up, he did as well.

Except... I slackened my pace suddenly and drifted towards the southern bank. Jonesy looked fooled, and I thought for a moment that he'd follow me. Then logic must have kicked in, because he stayed in the middle of the river. When we passed under the Prince's Highway Bridge, all three of us locked in a dead heat. Coach looked like he might have a heart attack.

He should have remembered that we'd studied the

river's currents and, when I accelerated after the next bend in the river, I felt a slight bump against the boat. I surged forward like a surfer who had just caught a massive wave. When the current took me back towards the river's center, I'd left everyone behind.

Matt had once told me it was a sweet thing to have the entire school cheering for him, and now I heard the cheers from the northern bank for me. With just two hundred yards to go, I had a fifty yard lead on Jonesy, and the other rower had faded out of the race. Almost effortlessly, I rowed past a large boat filled with V.I.P.s. A child played in its stern.

Someone should be watching her, I thought, as she climbed up the railing and tried to walk along it. It seemed inevitable when she toppled over and fell into the river. I waited to hear shouts, or see someone running, but no one seemed to have noticed her fall. Then, in slow motion, I saw her head pop up in the water and her arms flail as she tried to stay afloat.

Without thinking, I turned the boat and raced towards her. By the time I reached the spot, she was nowhere to be seen. I desperately looked around, but no one had missed her yet.

I pulled my shirt over my head, kicked my shoes off, and dove into the muddy water. I surfaced once, took another deep breath then dove again. This time my arm caught her dress. With my lungs straining for oxygen, I kicked for the surface, expecting to find boats nearby and people hovering to help. But the officials' boat was still in the distance, and Jonesy was rowing furiously for the finish line.

When I looked at the river bank, several people stood there talking on their mobiles. Obviously help was being summoned. I didn't know if I could wait.

The child whimpered and, when her teeth began chattering, I made up my mind. I lifted her into the dinghy and hauled myself back into it. After settling her on the bottom, I put my shirt around her, and sang lullabies as I headed back towards the finishing line. It was the only thing I could think of. Finishing the race wasn't the objective. I just wanted to get somewhere where she could be warm.

Just before I reached the finish, the officials' boat powered towards me. After crossing the line, I rowed to the dock, took the girl in my arms and staggered towards the tent to find Coach. He could handle everything. I just needed to puke the river out of my system and then sleep for a thousand years.

I'd only made it halfway when I saw the flashing lights of an ambulance, people with blankets and, thankfully, Coach rushing towards me.

"Damn fine thing, Compton," Coach said, as he bundled up the little girl and handed her over to a paramedic. He swaddled me in another blanket and began leading me to the ambulance as well.

"I'm fine, sir. I just need to rest. I don't need a hospital."

Chloe and Mr. Murray reached us just as I began arguing with Coach. "What's going on?" Mr. Murray demanded. "Thad, are you all right?"

"I'm fine. Tell them I don't need a hospital," I pleaded. "I just want to rest. I'm all right. Really."

Next to arrive was Frank Bundy. I watched as he shoved his way through spectators to the ambulance and, for a moment, didn't recognize him. His face was paper white and his hair looked like he'd been standing in tornado-force winds. He spoke to the paramedics, hugged the little girl, and then walked over. For some seconds, he stood silently while his Adam's apple worked furiously.

Finally he said, "I owe you more than I can ever repay, Thad. That was my little girl you saved. I know it cost you the $5,000 prize. I'll make that up to you, of course, and if there's anything else I can do, just let me know."

I felt my cheeks redden. I'd had no idea whose child it was. Even if I'd known that she was Ol' Bundy's descendant, I would have done the exact same thing. "Keep a better eye on her," I began and then realized that TV cameras were recording everything.

I turned my face away. "And, can you get those things turned off? I'm not someone special. I just did what I was supposed to. Anyone else would have done the same."

"But didn't," Frank Bundy said firmly. "Everyone else finished the race. Thad, thank you. I've got to get Cindy checked out right now, but I'll be in touch. Thanks."

With that he rushed off, and Chloe looked after him. "I wonder when he'll put two and two together."

Mr. Murray, who had walked over to speak with some of the television crew, now came back. "Thad, I've just promised that you will give a couple of interviews."

"No."

Mr. Murray took my shoulders and forced me to look into his eyes. "Thad, trust me. This is my business, after all. If you give a short press conference, everyone will be happy. If you don't, they'll try to get a story some way or another. This way, we control them. Okay?"

Chloe nodded her head. "That makes sense," she said and, after I refused again, she steamrollered on, "Thad, this is different. It's news. It's a feel-good story that everyone will want to know about. Do what Dad says."

I couldn't stop shivering as Mr. Murray went to arrange things. In the distance I heard applause. "What's going on?"

"It's the presentation ceremony. You should be up there getting the medal. Not Jonesy. It's a bloody shame you're not," Matt said, appearing suddenly. "Hi, Chloe."

"Hi, Matt. How did you get through security?"

"Told them I was Thad's brother," Matt replied with a grin that showed he was proud of his cunning. He looked at me, still huddled in the blanket, with concern. "That was a great race, Thad. Well done. No one could figure out why you stopped and started going backwards. I thought Coach would explode, but everyone's talking about it now. Do you want me to bring your bag over?"

Thad thought. "No, it's only got my trainers in it. Could you take it back to school? Mr. Murray said I can go back to Gran's."

"See ya, then." As he turned to go, Matt said casually, "Don't forget the dance, though."

"Where is it?" Chloe demanded.

"BLC," Matt said with a grin as he waved good-bye.

"BLC," Chloe muttered. "It's a school for vampires, vultures and behemoths."

I grinned when I saw the chagrin on Chloe's face. Beecroft Ladies College and Enderby were archrivals. Matt told stories about cat fights breaking out occasionally during their field hockey games. "Don't worry," I laughed, "I'll put a clove of garlic in my pocket."

"I don't understand why you have to go. Judy Thurston said her brother was coming home this weekend."

"It's a house dance. Their School House is hosting our School House. That's why we're stuck at school when everyone else is out."

"Come along you two," Mr. Murray said, preempting a response from Chloe. "Dr. Rivers has agreed that you can come back with us for a few hours. I'll take you to Majestic's studios and then back to school in time for the dance. It's too bad it's not a visiting weekend."

"Totally. Then he'd be safe from the weirdoes at

BLC," Chloe muttered.

When I arrived back at School House, I didn't want to see or talk to anyone. My body ached. I wasn't sure if it were from the race or the fight with Jonesy. As I changed from the navy dress suit I'd worn for the Majestic interview into my gray school slacks for the dance, I was tired, beyond fatigued tired. Matt, however, was full of energy.

"You were great on TV, Thad. Way, way better than Jonesy. I tell you, the whole school's proud of you. I heard Mr. Graham talking with Mr. Sutton, and he said you should get nominated for an honors' blazer. Jonesy's angry. Now that he's won the prize, everyone he owes money to has suddenly come to claim it. Nobody thinks he deserves it. Out of everyone in the school, you're the one who can always beat him somehow. You're his Hercules heel."

"Achilles," I corrected. "It's Achilles heel."

Matt shrugged. "Hercules, Achilles, whatever. Oh Thad, Majestic showed the end of the race just before your interview. It was great. There you were, rowing away, victory in the bag, then suddenly you're streaking off, going faster backwards than you'd been going frontwards. Freak-show. Then, you dove into the river for no apparent reason. I'm so proud you're my friend."

I didn't want to hear about it. "I only did what anyone would do." I thought for a moment. I didn't want to bring up a new subject, but I'd realized something when Mr. Murray was driving me back, and I had to get it done with. "I'm glad you're my friend, Matt. You're the real hero here. I told Mr. Murray that you'd called me a hypocrite because I'd stopped going to Chaplain Thomas's on Wednesdays."

Both of our faces were red, and I'd never really talked about stuff like this to anyone. Ever. It was one of those things. I knew that Matt wanted me to continue, but I owed him and today I'd learned how chancy things were in life. "Anyway, I told Mr. Murray what I'd told you. That I'd gotten way too busy. And then I had to apologize, because that was exactly the same reason he'd given me when we'd argued about church. You were right. I am a hypocrite."

Matt's face went even redder, and I knew he didn't talk like this either. "*Were* maybe. Anyway, let's get going. It will be detentions if Mr. Graham has to send someone to get us."

As the bus wended its way through BLC's grounds, I noticed that the Beecroft school buildings looked more modern than Enderby's, but they were equally magnificent. No wonder boys like Matt needed scholarships to go to school.

Then we walked into the BLC's auditorium, and I became even more embarrassed than I'd been when talking to Matt. It seemed that every girl stood and applauded, and it took several seconds before I realized that I was the reason.

I didn't know what to do. Mr. Graham edged closer and hissed, "Do something."

Okay, but what? I nodded my head when a couple of girls praised me and felt stupid. Then I ducked behind Matt and muttered, "Don't leave me."

"Have to. Don't forget, we're here to dance."

Continuous dancing followed, and I felt like I'd rather row across the Pacific than dance with one more girl. Even seniors had cut in on the slow dances. A different one every three seconds. Finally, I had enough. I excused myself and walked across to Matt. "I need to pee. Where is it?"

When we came back, Matt steered me over to the food area. "I'll get food. You line up for drinks."

Getting drinks was easy, if embarrassing. I nodded thanks when one of the BLC teachers poured them and offered more congratulations, then scurried back to Matt. "It's a nightmare. Everyone knows who I am."

Matt laughed. "You shouldn't have gone around being a hero. It's your own fault, so stop whining. Here, have a sandwich. They're pretty good."

I'd no sooner put the sandwich in my mouth when there was a drum roll and the head of BLC School House took the microphone from the DJ. "Welcome, Dubbees. We're pleased to be hosting you on this very special night. And now, if you please, a round of applause of the hero of the day, Thad Compton."

I thought my face should just go red and stay red. I was sick of being embarrassed. Matt giggled as he pushed me into the center of the room towards the teacher. I shook her hand, thanked her politely. Total shock nailed my feet to the floor when she went on, "Age has its privileges, and now I claim one. Thad, may I have the honor of this dance?"

Dead. I knew I was dead once this got around King William's on Monday.

The dance was a slow one with a 1-2-3 beat. I could shuffle around the floor as well as anyone else. But, with the head? After I heard a few snickers from the Dubbees behind me, I thought what the heck. I put my arm around her, took her hand in mine and started waltzing. I could feel the shock as easily as a river current, and gradually I realized we were the only ones on the floor.

When the music finished, I escorted her back to her chair, bowed, and headed back to the food and drink section. Matt wasn't there, and neither was his plate of food. I almost picked up my drink, when something Tyce Dellman had said popped into my mind. "Never, ever, drink from your glass at a party once you've left it. Promise me."

I walked away, fed up with the whole night. I hated being conspicuous, hated being praised for doing something that should have been thought of as normal. I was tired, cranky and I couldn't find Matt. Instead I looked for Mr.

Graham. If saving Cindy Bundy had been worthwhile and I was such a hero, surely he'd let me rest in the bus.

I found him talking on his mobile. Before I could say anything, he frowned. "What is it, Thad? Luke's in charge now. My daughter's had an accident, and I need to go home and get my wife over to the hospital."

"Sir? Could I come with you? To school? I can't take this anymore."

Mr. Graham hesitated for a few seconds before punching a number on his mobile. He listened for a while and frowned again, "Luke's not picking up, and I don't want to wade through the dancers to get him." When Luke's phone obviously clicked through to voice mail, Mr. Graham spoke rapidly. After putting his own phone back in his pocket, he walked towards a waiting taxi. "Come along, Thad. Don't keep me waiting."

18

I was watching an old Wolverine movie and just about jumped out of my skin when Luke burst into the junior common room. After that one look at him, I knew that something was seriously wrong. His clothes were rumpled, his tie halfway was around his neck. Worse, he looked desperately worried.

"You're here."

"I got permission to leave the dance early. I came across with Mr. Graham. He texted you. What's wrong? I'm not in trouble, am I?"

"What? No, no. Turn the movie off, will you?"

My fears escalated when Luke flung himself into an armchair beside me. Only something important would bring him into the junior room. "What's wrong? What's going on?"

"You don't know how lucky you are that you left Beecroft when you did." He seemed to search for words for a few moments, and then he put his arm on mine. "Thad, there's no easy way to say this. Bruce Jones put a drug into your drink. He'd arranged for one of his BLC friends to dress you like a girl with make-up and everything and leave you under some bushes. You would have been found in the morning, looking absolutely stupid, and having no idea of what happened.

Tyce had made me look up the date rape drug

Rohypnol on the internet. "A roofie? Jonesy tried to give me a roofie? Why would he do that?"

Luke shrugged. "Who knows?"

"A friend made me promise that I'd never, ever, drink out of a glass at a party once I'd left it. After I danced with their head, I saw my glass had been moved, so I left it."

"It's a pity Matt Peters doesn't have the same friend. He must have mistaken your glass for his. He drank the drug instead."

I felt horror, then pure pulsating rage. I jumped to my feet, my hands bunched into fists. "I'll kill Jonesy for this. Hasn't he any sense? Someone will get seriously hurt one day."

"Your some day is right now, Thad. You don't know the worst of it. The doctor suspects that Matt's allergic to it. They're fighting for his life right now in the infirmary. A helicopter's gone to pick up his mother. It's a real horror show. The police are involved. Jones will be lucky if he's only expelled. He'll be charged, for sure."

"What can I do?"

Again Luke shrugged. "Pray? I only stopped by to tell you where Matt is. Anyway, I've got to go with Dr. Rivers and meet the chopper. This is absolutely the worst night of my life."

Luke left, and I slumped back in my chair. Luke was right. Prayer *was* the only thing I could do. I pushed myself forward and had begun to concentrate when there was a quiet knock on the door.

Jonesy came in. A Jonesy I'd never seen. Although dressed immaculately, he looked broken. "I've only a moment," he said quietly. "I've come to apologize. I can't believe I did it, can't believe I thought it would be a good joke. I'm sorry, Compton. Really sorry for everything that's happened from the first time I knocked you down. I'm being arrested, but it's not because of that. I really am sorry. I'd give anything, absolutely anything, for the chance to do it all over again."

There was another knock on the door, and when Jonesy opened it, I saw the police in the hallway.

I walked back to my room thinking hard about Jonesy. He seemed totally sincere. I believed him—that he would give anything to do everything differently. At least, right now. Right now under arrest in a police car.

I couldn't do anything for him, even if I wanted to. But there was something I could do for Matt. He'd need clothes. I hated hospital gowns. They were uncomfortable and embarrassing. I found Matt's shorts, tee shirts, the book he was reading and toiletries. Then I put them, plus a toothbrush and a comb, into his pack and set off for the infirmary.

Without Mr. Graham or Luke around, School House was chaos. Groups of boys clustered together, talking in low voices. They watched, but no one said anything as I broke one of the major rules and opened the front door after midnight. Everything was quieter outside, but I saw flashing lights in the Infirmary area.

I acted like I'd been told to bring Matt's clothes over, so nobody stopped me when I entered it. But when I walked towards the room I thought Matt might be in, Dr. Rivers walked out of it. He looked like he'd aged ten years. His hair was mussed, his shoulders slumped. Even his mouth sloped downwards.

"What on earth are you doing here, Thad?"

"Bringing Matt's things."

"Come over here." Dr. Rivers took Matt's pack and indicated a couple of chairs near the entrance.

I sat, thinking I'd get a lecture for being out of my room. Dr. Rivers didn't see angry, though. Just sad. I looked at the lights outside, flashing red and white with monotonous regularity. I couldn't understand everything that had happened, but the police presence appalled me and might account for Dr. Rivers' sorrow. He seemed so sad, that I wanted to comfort him, but I realized that hugging my headmaster was probably not my best option. And so, the silence stretched.

Eventually Dr. Rivers sat straighter. "Thad. You're going to need your strength. Matt's gone. He went into extreme anaphylactic shock on the bus coming back from BLC and didn't come out of it. The doctor pronounced him dead about fifteen minutes ago."

I heard the words, but I couldn't process them. It wasn't just the anaphylactic shock I didn't get. It was the whole package. Matt couldn't be dead. He was one of the fittest guys in the school.

Dead.

It might have been me, and I tried hard to listen as Dr. Rivers rambled on about what would happen next. Jonesy had meant that drug for me. Now, my brave, funny friend was dead because he hadn't smelt danger at a school dance.

I bent my head, unable to absorb it. If I hadn't seen the genuine sorrow in Jonesy's eyes, I'd go wherever he was and thrash the daylights out of him. That wasn't an option, but I didn't know what else was. Ignoring Dr. Rivers, I stumbled to my feet and lurched out the door.

What exactly had happened? Jonesy had tried to make me look stupid, but his prank had gone wrong with hideous consequences for Matt. I huddled against the roots of a gum tree and sobbed. I'd only known Matt for a couple of months, yet he'd become my best friend, except for Chloe.

Time after time Matt's quick intelligence had stopped me from making a fool of myself. Somehow he'd understood that I hadn't known what to do. He'd had the courage to face down Jonesy and friends, then use his humor to spin it into a funny story.

Matt had always had my back.

When would my losses end? I'd cried this hard in the London jail after I'd been caught stealing and for my mother once I knew I'd never see her again. On the ship to New South Wales, I'd turned my face to the wall so none of the others would see my tears and think I was easy prey.

I'd been too sick in the beginning to mourn leaving 1833. Only after I'd got better had I felt the agonizing loss of the Kendricks and Preacher Dan. And what about Chloe and Mr. White? Would I lose them too?

Once I stopped feeling sorry for myself, I walked around the grounds. Nothing changed. Anger swirled round my mind like the fog in London. During my worst times with Ol' Bundy, I used to crawl under some stairs and wonder why I'd been born. Now, I wondered why Chloe had brought me forward to her world. Would she have done it if she'd known the cost would be Matt's life?

I'd have to tell her. For the first time I was glad that she was home in Double Bay, not at Enderby this weekend. I pulled out my mobile out and squinted at the time. 2:35. Too bloody thirty-five bad. I speed-dialed her number and prayed that she'd answer.

"Oh, my God!" she exclaimed when I told her the news. I heard her phone clatter to the floor, and her sobs as she picked it up. "Thad, I'm so sorry," she hiccupped. "What happened exactly?"

"Jonesy."

Her anger boiled over once she heard the details. "I hate Jonesy, and every one of his smirky friends. I hope they get boils all over themselves, and that someone lances them with a rusty knife. I hope they get septicemia and their pricks fall off."

She rattled off several other horrible medical disasters she wished would happen until she stopped suddenly in mid-sentence. "Oh, Thad. It's so horrible, and I know what good friends you and he were. What can I do? Do you want to come here? Do you want me to wake Dad up so that he can come and get you?"

If she'd said Wahmurra, it would have been different. Double Bay wasn't really my home. "Could you come here? I need someone to talk to right now. Maybe in the morning we can go to Wahmurra."

Silence. I could almost hear her thinking. I sort of knew what I was asking. It was a long way, especially in the early morning hours. Also risky. We'd probably both be expelled if anyone found us together on the school grounds. On the other hand, who could possibly care with everything else that was happening?

"Sure. I'll get a taxi," she finally said, and judging by the rustling sounds, she'd already started getting her things together. "I'll get there in about an hour."

"I'll meet you in the turning circle. Give me a call when you're about five minutes away."

"What will you do till then?"

"Go to the chapel. I don't want to go back to my room. I don't want to talk to anyone, and I'm too wound up to sleep. Bye."

The chapel was cold. I lit the chancel candles and wrapped a couple of the altar cloths around myself. They were about ten feet long and beautifully embroidered on one side with gold silk, but the felt underside was as warm as a blanket. I knew somebody would think it sacrilegious, but I doubted that God would.

God would think Matt's death sacrilegious.

I sat on the altar steps, my chest heaving as I remembered Matt and the shy smile that curled his mouth when he gave the punch line to some of his jokes. I, too, smiled a tiny bit at the memory of Matt, when he'd gathered up his courage to tell me that he was a Dubbee only because of a Compton scholarship

It wasn't fair!

I wanted to pound the altar. Where was God? Why hadn't he protected Matt? Matt was one of his good guys. Why hadn't God looked out for him?

I don't know when my thoughts became angry, direct questions. All I knew was that I was suddenly kneeling and sobbing my anguish and questions out. Again. Matt had always guarded my back. Why hadn't I'd done the same for him? I was Jonesy's target and, like Jonesy, I'd do anything now to undo the past.

You can, a voice whispered.

I jumped to my feet and whirled around. When I saw no one, I walked down the aisle, searching everywhere. Defeated, and wondering if I were delusional, I returned to the front pew.

You can.

This time I didn't bother turning around. I just concentrated on working out what I could do. I gloomed, thought, gloomed, and suddenly sat up. I don't know exactly where the idea came from, but I had a plan.

If anyone had been watching, my actions would have looked like those of a madman, because I started touching every stone in the wall on my side of the chapel. It had been beautifully designed by one of Australia's best architects. I knew that Billy had left money in a trust fund, so that when the school moved from Parramatta in the 1920s, the builders had incorporated parts of the original chapel into the present one. I'd read about it while I was in the infirmary.

I had just started on the other wall when my phone rang. Chloe was five minutes away. But, as I ran to the turning circle, my mind concentrated on Billy and his messages.

Once she stepped out from the car, I grabbed Chloe and hugged her. "Thanks for coming. I worried whether a taxi might refuse to bring you here at this time of night. I never thought you'd get a limo," I said, taking her hand and leading her to a nearby bench.

"I didn't chance a taxi, so I phoned the service Dad uses and put it on his account. It gave me sudden respectability. Plus, I told the driver Dad was meeting us here. I don't know if he believed me. He gave me his card in case of trouble," she told him. Then she turned and took a long look at my face. "What's happened to you, though? I thought you'd be in the doldrums of despair."

"I am."

"You don't look it."

"Well, I was. But Chloe, listen. I've had an idea."

"And?"

I buried my hands into my pockets. "I've been thinking. I didn't tell you, but one of the most extraordinary things is that Jonesy apologized before the police took him away."

"Jonesy? Apologize? Does he know how to," Chloe exclaimed, the very tone of her voice showing disgust.

"Apparently. But Chloe, I'd swear on a stack of Bibles he was genuine, that he was telling the truth. He said he'd do anything for a second chance."

"Like sell his soul to the devil?"

"I don't know. Maybe he would. He's not entirely bad. I've seen him do one, maybe two, decent things since I've been here."

"Big deal." Chloe blew on her fingers and stuffed them back into the pockets of her fleece. May wasn't really winter in Sydney, but it obviously felt like it to her. "Hurry up, Thad. I'm going to die of cold if we stay here." Once she realized what she'd said, she looked stricken. "Sorry. Wasn't thinking."

"That's all right."

"Come on, Thad. What's your big idea? We can't stay here all night."

"You're right." I stood up and stamped my feet to restore circulation. "Come on. Let's go."

"Where?"

"The chapel." I stamped my feet again and pulled her up. "Come on. Let's go. You can listen to my idea on the way and tell me if it's crazy."

"It's crazy. I know it."

About half way to the chapel, I looked across to the infirmary. The emergency vehicles had long gone, and there were only a couple of cars still around. I knew there was no time to waste, so when I spoke, I know I sounded desperate. "Chloe, when I was in the chapel, something started me wishing I could redo tonight somehow, and I remembered Billy insisting that there was more than one way between his world and this. It seemed the most important thing he wanted me to know, so I asked myself why. Why did he emphasize it?"

"Probably because he knew you had to go back sometime," Chloe answered.

"But, Chloe, what if *this* is the time? If anyone should have died, it's me. I'm the one who should be dead. Not, Matt. He drank the drug I was supposed to take. I feel I owe him."

"That's ridiculous. First off, you don't know that you would have had the same reaction Matt had." Chloe looked at me, her eyes troubled. "You're wrong, Thad. Totally wrong. There's only Jonesy to blame, and I'm glad the police have him."

"So am I. But this is what I've been thinking. What if I

find the way that Billy keeps telling me exists, and I take Matt to Billy's time?"

"Back to Wahmurra? I don't think it works like that," Chloe told me, her voice sounding troubled.

"But, who knows? We're the only people who've time travelled."

"That we know about," Chloe corrected.

"Okay, yes. But, tell me. Why wouldn't my idea work? You brought me here so I'd supposedly have a better life. What's wrong with trying to save Matt? Think about it. Every time it's happened, you always arrived earlier than when you left. That's why you've had two Speech Days. If I take Matt, we'll arrive before he died. When I bring him back, he'll arrive before the dance. That way he won't drink the drug, and Jonesy will get his second chance."

"Wouldn't it be easier if you went by yourself and came back before the dance? Then you could stay around to make sure Matt doesn't drink it."

"But things aren't always duplicated. You won two prizes at Speech Day this time, not the one you said you got before. Your dad came across for your birthday this time. He didn't before. Look, we don't know for sure that it would work, but I feel in my gut that I have to try. I can't let Matt be buried without doing anything."

Chloe slumped against me, lost in thought. "I don't know," she said, her voice full of doubt. "But if your plan has to have a chance, we have to get Matt out of the infirmary before the autopsy people arrive."

Relieved by the thought of action, I ran towards the infirmary. "Come on, let's hurry."

"Just think," Chloe panted as she raced to keep up with me. "I might have been peacefully having nightmares in bed."

19

The infirmary seemed subdued. Somehow the brightness of the emergency vehicles had leached all color from the walls, leaving them grey. The only sound now was the wind rustling the leaves of the gum trees by the front door. They seemed to droop in desolation, as though they wept in despair over humanity's stupidity.

As Chloe and I watched from the shadows, Dr. Rivers led Matt's mother out towards his car. There was no doubting her grief—she seemed to have shrunk five inches from the day we'd met her at Michael Dee's. "I feel sorry for her," Chloe said as the car drove off. "Her son is dead. I wonder what she'd say about your crazy idea."

"She'd say go for it. What mother wouldn't?"

As Chloe walked towards the front door, I jerked her back. "We can't go in that way. If Matron's at her desk, she'll see us. It's best if I go in through the side door. I'll look around and signal you when it's all right."

"While I wait and freeze in the cold? No thanks," Chloe muttered as she raced after me.

"Then shut up and do what I say."

Chloe muttered something more but obediently followed. Matt was in a room towards the back on the ground floor, and I stared at the body in its blue and white hospital gown. Matt's face had no color. It looked like someone had erased every sign of his fourteen years of life from it. Gone were the laugh lines that bracketed his mouth and the crinkles around his eyes. His cowlick wasn't sticking up from his head defiantly. It, too, had lost its life.

Looking at my friend, I felt an incredible burst of tenderness. Then reality took over. "You stay put," I told Chloe in a stage whisper. "I'll find a wheelchair. That's the only way we can get him over to the chapel."

"To the chapel? Why?"

"Later," I whispered and braved the hallway again.

"Now I know what dead weight means," I muttered moments later while I tried to fit Matt into a wheelchair.

"That's because rigor mortis is setting in," Chloe panted as she heaved as well. "Come on, Matt. Cooperate," she exhorted illogically. "This is for your own good."

"Sssh. I hear Matron."

"We're all dead, if she comes in," Chloe muttered.

"Then it's three of us she'll have to deal with," I whispered, then stopped. Part of me understood, but the other part was appalled by our gallows humor. "Sorry, Matt. No disrespect. I'm spooked and can't stop myself."

We held our breath while Matron's footsteps came closer and closer, then faded after she passed by. "That's too close for comfort. Let's get out of here."

Not wanting to risk anything, I steered the wheelchair towards the back door, explaining, "She's more likely to be near the front if she's waiting for people."

It was slow going. The wheelchair wasn't designed for gravel walkways. It was worse when we cut across grass. When we hit a rut, Matt toppled to the ground. It took an astounding amount of strength to reposition him into the chair.

"I'm using muscles I didn't know I had," Chloe grumbled.

I didn't know about muscles, but I felt the events of the day catching up on me. I'd been worn out after the boat race, then dog-tired at the dance. Matt's death and this rescue exhausted every bit of emotional energy I had.

Once we carried the wheelchair up the chapel steps, we were almost too fatigued to go further. "Now what?" Chloe asked.

"Rest," I said, sitting down on the nearest pew. "Chloe, think back to when you found the yellow brick. Was there anything strange about it, other than the thumbprint?"

"Do you mean were there flashing lights? Did it pulse or something?"

After I nodded, she went on. "As soon as I put my hand on it, I heard voices from the past. Mom heard them too. Not the same ones, of course. She said that when she touched the pew, she heard voices asking God for a doctor."

I nodded. "I think there's a way to my world from this chapel. That's the reason Billy repeated himself time and time again about there being more than one way between our worlds."

Chloe looked worried. "There can't be that many. If there were, everyone would know about them."

"Think about it. We know Billy's not stupid, but his letters went on and on about there being more ways. We know there's the yellow brick that worked for you, the pew in Preacher Dan's church that your mother used, and Billy says there's one in your boat house."

"That's three. But, don't you see? There's a connection. Wahmurra."

"Okay." I thought for a moment, while Chloe wrapped an altar cloth more tightly against her. "Listen, Chloe. What if one of those ways was the old chapel at King William's when it was in Parramatta? Billy would know from Lady Peter that it would be moved. There's your

Wahmurra connection. Maybe that's why he paid for certain parts to be brought here when the school moved. He was making sure I'd be able to use a time-gate when I came to school here."

Chloe got up and wheeled Matt's wheelchair further into the chapel while she thought. "I suppose it makes sense. But, we don't have much time. I think we have to get Matt to Wahmurra as fast as possible—if we're going through with your plan. I still think it would be easier if you went by yourself, though."

"What if I came back later though? After the dance? He'd still be dead."

"Well, at least you would have tried. What worse can happen to him?"

I shrugged, and Chloe apparently saw that it was useless to argue. "Right," she said. "I'm going to give you fifteen minutes to find your time-gate. If you can't, I'll phone Dad and beg for the biggest favor ever. He'll go spare, but I'll ask him to drive the three of us to Wahmurra. If you can't find Billy's way, we'll try the yellow brick."

I was already scanning the chapel. "Billy wouldn't have used stones which would be inaccessible, or ones which might be accidentally pushed against. I've already tried this wall. As far as I know, the outer wall in the side chapel was built from Parramatta stone." I ran across to it and began touching as many stones as I could.

Chloe looked around. "What about the window?"

The east window of the chapel was renowned for its extraordinary glass. The lower part showed Mary and Martha crying while their neighbors comforted them. They seemed oblivious to Jesus, who was raising the dead Lazarus to life. For a stained glass window from the nineteenth century, it showed rare motion in the faces. The women's faces exposed their grief over the loss of a much loved brother. The face of Jesus revealed love for a dear friend. It was no wonder that hundreds of people came to see it whenever King William's had a viewing day.

I hurried over to it. "This makes sense, doesn't it? The resurrection thing, I mean. But, there aren't any stone blocks around it. There's just the delicate bits keeping it together."

"Let's try," Chloe suggested. "Time's running out."

I pressed every bit of stone I could reach. "Maybe it's the glass," I told Chloe, reaching up to press lightly against the ruby-red glass of Martha's dress, then the blue of Mary's. I ran my fingers over the green grass the sisters knelt on, and as soon as one finger touched the robe of Jesus, I jerked back.

"This is it. I could hear Preacher Dan. Wait here while I run back to get clothes for Matt. He cannot go back into the nineteenth century in a hospital gown!"

Chloe shouted something, but I raced across the campus as fast as I could. I kept to the shadows, but always took the fastest way. Back in our room, I hurriedly stuffed shorts and shirts, trainers and socks into a pack, and then more carefully packed both our uniforms. I threw the pack out the window and reached back for my boater. Old habits die hard, and Dubbees always wore the thing when off campus. Besides, I wanted to show my uniform to Lord and Lady Peter Kendricks.

Chloe glared when I arrived back at the chapel. "You have no idea what I've been going through," she stormed. "It was Stephen King spooky, Thad. It was all right when you were here and I could keep thinking about Matt as Matt. But once you left, all I could think about was his body. His dead body. Don't ever leave me alone with a dead body again. Promise."

I didn't grin, but only because I could see she'd been

really scared. "Chloe, remember it's Matt. Besides. I've seen lots of dead bodies. On the boat out and even at Wahmurra. You've got to remember that a dead body can't hurt you."

"But they can, Thad. There's all sorts of diseases you can get from them. That's why people wear gloves when they touch them," Chloe retorted, remembering things her doctor mother had taught her.

"Forget that, for now, will you? I think someone's worked out that Matt's missing. There were shouts and I heard a siren a couple of minutes ago."

She started pushing the wheelchair closer to the stained glass window, she took time for one last threat. "Remember this, Thad Compton. I will never, ever, forgive you for leaving me here alone. Never. What's more, I've thought of all kinds of punishments for you."

"Save them up for when I get back, will you?"

"When you get back? I'm coming with you."

"Chloe, you can't. You know it's dangerous. I almost died last time."

"That's exactly why I have to go with you. Think, Thad. What if this works for Matt, but not for you? He'd be stuck in 1833, not knowing anyone and not knowing what happened to him. He'd never get back. This way, if anything happened to you, I can bring him back."

"But it's dangerous," I protested. "Look, Chloe. Be logical. Matt's already dead, so if it doesn't work, he can't be worse off. And, me? I know I can't go back to 1833 and live as a convict. I've changed too much. But I don't feel that I belong here either. There's always stuff happening that I don't know about or can't predict. What's more, if anything happened to you, think of your dad and Gran. They'd be devastated."

Chloe looked troubled. "I know. I sent Dad a long text while you were gone. I told him how much I loved him, and why I felt I had to do this." She rubbed tears from her eyes angrily. "Come on, Thad. There's no time to waste. For every reason you have, I have another. We can argue until the sky falls down, so let's do it."

"Okay, but how? Carry him through the window, or keep him in the chair?"

"I have no idea. Carry him, I think."

"Right. Okay, let's get him to the window. You keep him draped over me while I push against it."

It was much harder work than it had been half an hour earlier. Rigor mortis had advanced, and the body didn't want to straighten up. We eventually managed to get Matt slumped over my shoulder and then we half-dragged, half-carried him to the window.

"Chloe, hold on tight," I ordered, reaching upwards to the glass window. "Ready?"

20

I felt like I'd dropped a million feet. A thousand voices rang in my ears, even when I shook my head to get rid of them. I was in a small, box-like room built from saplings nailed together. A little light filtered in through the cracks and, as my eyes adjusted to its gloom, I saw a sleeping platform and knew where I was.

This was the hut that I'd built back in 1833. I saw my tin basin, a jug and a mug on a shelf. Apart from an accumulation of dust, nothing had changed, and I wondered if I'd dreamed the past months and was still a convict. Only after my tongue explored my teeth and found braces, did I know for sure that I'd switched worlds again.

I looked around desperately. I could hear Chloe throwing up somewhere and part of me settled immediately. It always did when I was with her. Then I saw a body across the room. Matt. Was he still dead? Had switching worlds worked? With a great deal of trepidation, I walked across the small room, and stretched my hand out to touch the body.

I couldn't do it. I froze with my fingertips just inches away. Somehow, I'd used up my courage quotient for the night. Only Chloe stumbling outside unfroze me. My fingers trembled as I touched Matt's neck and searched for a pulse.

Nothing.

The knowledge that I'd failed seeped through me.

Chloe and I had done this mad dash through time, upsetting whatever laws that governed time and space, for nothing. As I turned away to help Chloe, I realized something. Matt's neck hadn't been cold, and his body wasn't in the funny still position anymore.

I spun around, and this time my hand eagerly searched Matt's neck until I found a thin, erratic pulse. Then I threw myself onto the dirt floor beside my old bed in thankfulness. Matt still had a chance.

"I'm going for Lady Peter," I told Chloe as I rushed outside a minute later. "Let's pray she isn't in Sydney."

Once I reached the entrance to the House, I slowed down. The last thing anyone needed was for Billy and Polly to wake up and go on and on about dead sailor boys as they had when Chloe arrived. I crept past the doorway of Billy's room and knocked softly once I reached the master bedroom.

Lord Peter's eyes nearly popped out in astonishment when he opened the door. I quickly held a finger to my lips. "Lady Peter? Is she here?"

"Thad?" she answered, and I heard her searching for clothes in the near darkness. Then Lord Peter lit a candle, and I realized they had aged. It seemed time had stood still in Chloe's century, but had accelerated in theirs.

Lady Peter touched my face, smiled when she saw the braces, and then quickly asked, "Chloe? Is she here? Is she well?"

"Throwing up her dinner outside my hut, my lady." I said and wasn't surprised by her look of intense happiness.

"Come on, Peter," she called out softly. "Let's go."

"You need your medical bag," I told her. "We've brought you a patient. He's very sick, and it's very complicated."

"Must be, if you think I'm better than twentieth-first

century medicine."

When we reached the hut, Chloe had managed to clean herself up. At the sight of her mother, she whooped, ran, and hugged her fiercely. "I didn't think I'd ever see you again," she said over and over, with tears rolling down her face.

Keeping her close with an arm, Lady Peter looked at me. "Where's the patient?"

"Here," I answered and took the candle so that she could see Matt.

Lady Peter quickly transformed into Dr. Christina Murray, her twenty-first century self. She knelt beside Matt, ran her hands over him, acquiring as much knowledge as she could. "He's desperately ill," she said finally. "I don't know that I'll be much good. Why on earth did you bring him here?"

Chloe laughed semi-hysterically. "He's a lot better than he was a couple of hours ago. Mom, you have to be able to save him."

"I'll get some tree bark tea into him for a start," Lady Peter said. "Peter, can you and Thad carry him into the spare bedroom in our wing? I don't want the children becoming upset. Chloe, wake Nurse. Tell her I need bark tea and hot compresses immediately."

By mid-morning, Matt's condition hadn't changed. To some extent that was good news. He was alive, even though he clung to life by the barest sliver of a fingernail. Lady Peter sat by his bed giving him small sips of a tea. Chloe and I huddled across the room, willing him to respond. After some time, Lady Peter pushed the teapot aside. "Bark tea can do only so much. There's just one more thing I can think of, and it's a long shot. Someone will have to ask Preacher Dan to find Jimmy Bones."

"I'll go," Billy said, and only then did we see him

and Polly in the doorway, their eyes wide as they stared at me and then Chloe.

They seemed to be about seven or eight. Other than their height, they hadn't changed much. Their eyes still had a look of intense interest in everything, and they carried themselves with an air of independence.

Lady Peter didn't seem to turn a hair at their sudden appearance and offer to go to the work yards. "Quickly then, Billy," she ordered. "And make sure you come straight back here without talking to anyone. Promise?"

"Who's Jimmy Bones?" Chloe asked when they ran off.

"What will we tell them about us?" I asked. "You saw the questions in their eyes."

"Later, Thad. Right now, I want you to tell me everything you can about your friend. Everything, Thad."

When I told what had happened to Matt, Lady Peter's expression went from disgust, to sorrow that Matt had died, and incredulity that we had brought him into her world. "It's outrageous," she scolded us. "What were you thinking? You know it's not supposed to work like that."

I looked back at her. "The point, my lady, is that we don't know. And, you can't deny that it worked."

"Somewhat," she snapped. "I hope you haven't condemned him to be a vegetable here. Anyway, let's leave that for now and work out what we're going to tell Billy and Polly about you."

After we came up with a story about us coming back from a very long trip that we thought the twins would accept, Chloe asked again about Jimmy Bones.

Lady Peter waited as Mrs. Grant, the housekeeper, brought a bowl of warm water so that she could sponge Matt down. "Jimmy Bones is the native medicine man," she told us when she finished. "He and I have just begun to make friends. We're a mutual aid society. He brings me medicines and oils from plants and bushes, as well as people he can't help. Now, I'm returning the favor."

It took several hours for Dan to find Jimmy Bones. During that time Matt's condition didn't change, so Lord and Lady Peter took the opportunity to catch up. Lord Peter was fascinated by everything and particularly about my life at King William's. Lady Peter cried when she heard stuff about Mr. Murray and Gran. "It's the world I've lost. I'm just thankful I can see you one more time," she told Chloe.

Just before lunch, Mrs. Grant arrived with 1830s clothes. "These are yours from last time," she said to Chloe, running a critical eye over her. "You haven't grown much." Getting clothing for me had been a bigger problem. "I altered some of Mr. White's," she announced. "Seeing that he's in Tamworth, he can't object. But, if you're still here when he comes back, I won't be responsible, Thad. He'll feed you to the sharks."

As everyone smiled, she reached out and hugged me. "Welcome back. As soon as you're respectable, Cook wants to see you. Says she's baked you a special pie. Now, I don't want to know where you've been or how you got here but, young Thad, it does my heart good to see you looking so well."

I was glad that Mr. White was away. I'd grown to love the twenty-first century Mr. White, but I still had huge doubts about the 1830's version. That Mr. White had once tried to kill Chloe and me. Later though, when I dressed in Mr. White's altered jacket and trousers, I realized exactly how much I'd changed.

Before I'd gone into the twenty-first century, I'd never have dreamed of wearing the overseer's clothes. Now that I was used to Armani jackets, I looked at Mr. White's clothes with a critical eye. The tailoring was superb, but they felt tight and scratchy.

Luncheon merely confirmed this sense of change. It was taken for granted that I'd eat with the family. In 1833, I would have been punished if I'd even stepped into the dining room without permission.

Strangely I felt quite at home conversing with Lord Peter, handing condiments to Chloe, and being waited on by the maid. I wanted to shout, *I'm a convict. That's my excuse for a hut out there beyond the kitchen garden.*

But the truth was that I wasn't treated as a convict and I didn't behave as one. I ate and acted as a student from King William's School for Boys. The only identity I had left, I gloomed later, was that of a Dubbee.

Matt seemed much the same when we went back to the sickroom. Mrs. Grant had managed to get more of the tannin-rich tea into him, and she reported happily that he had tried to stop her giving him more. I stuck a finger into the brew and was immediately on Matt's side. The tea was totally disgusting.

Encouraged by this small act of defiance, Chloe and I stayed with Matt, talking softly and trying to include him in our conversations. Lady Peter visited the room constantly. "He should be in a proper hospital," she fretted. "He needs drips and tests. I could do so much more for him there."

"Mom," Chloe interjected. "He was in a hospital, remember? It didn't help."

Time really seemed to stand still. We felt we couldn't leave Matt. In any case, no one had been able to come up with a story to explain me to those outside the Kendricks' house. I'd still be recognized by anyone on the huge estate, and I could imagine the questions.

What had happened to my limp? Why did I have braces on my teeth? Why did I look only an inch or so taller when I'd been gone for three years? While Chloe could tell people she was another relative of Lady Peter's, my differences couldn't be easily explained.

When footsteps sounded outside, everyone breathed a sigh of relief. Lady Peter went out to greet Dan and Jimmy Bones, and for several moments we listened to the conversation with varying degrees of amusement. Dan had obviously tried to learn Jimmy's language, and I thought his grasp of it was much the same as Jimmy's knowledge of English.

The door opened, and I stood up. Jimmy paused in the entrance. He was smaller than Chloe and as skinny as a supermodel. His straggly beard was divided into two, like an elongated W. I bit back a laugh when I saw his trousers. They looked exactly like the ones I'd left behind. Jimmy hadn't bothered with a shirt, although he'd festooned his arms with amulets. He had a large pouch on a string around his neck, and his right hand was firmly attached to a lethal-looking spear.

His eyes darted back and forth between Chloe and me for several long seconds. Then he seemed to steel himself, looked across the room at Matt, and shuddered violently. For several long seconds he stood trembling, his eyes closed, his head shaking from one side to the other. After another quick look, he howled like a terrified animal until, with his spear held out in front of him, he raced out of the house.

21

Lady Peter rushed after the men. We hurried to the window and stuck our heads out to listen. At any other time, I might have laughed. When Jimmy spoke, his left hand gesticulated wildly while his right hand thumped the spear into the ground. Dan pleaded; Jimmy shouted back. When Dan increased his volume; Jimmy shouted louder. Eventually Dan walked over to Lady Peter.

"He won't go back into the room. Not for anything," he told her. Jimmy Bones launched into another feverish explanation that Dan tried to translate. "He says it's full of things that shouldn't be there. Bad things that could catch his soul and throw it into the middle of the water. Spirits, he says. Bad spirits."

Lady Peter held her hands out to Jimmy, "What about the boy? Can you help him? Can you suggest something? Anything?"

Jimmy Bones exploded into yet another torrent of words. Preacher Dan stopped him every now and then to ask questions that Jimmy answered at full velocity. When he finally wound down, he took an amulet off his arm, handed it to Lady Peter, then reached into the pouch around his neck.

Taking out some dried herbs, he put them in Lady Peter's hand, "Ver' strong. Kill most fella. Not young fella in there. He already dead boy." He stopped, looked behind at the sickroom and gave a strange laugh. "Put in tea," he continued, holding up a miniscule amount. "Put and see. Try again, Right, missus?" Then he turned to Dan and continued in his own language, before exploding into another eerie sound and speeding off into the bushes.

When Preacher Dan looked at Lady Peter, he seemed worried. "He insists there's things in the sickroom that shouldn't be here. Bad spirits. That's what's wrong with the boy. It's spiritual warfare, he says. Good against evil. If it happened in his camp, they would put clay around the boy and paint a skeleton on top on it. That way, his soul would know where it belonged and not get lost. Then he and his elders would dance and chant all night. He says to take care of the spirits first, and the body second."

We looked at each other, our heads still out of the window. Healing Matt had seemed relatively simple on the bench back at King William's. To some extent Jimmy's diagnosis made sense.

"What's really wrong with Matt?"

"Why does everyone, except Jimmy, talk about him in whispers?"

We swiveled around to see Billy and Polly standing behind us. "You two," I exploded, taking out my frustrations on them. "You're as much trouble now as you used to be." After their faces crumbled and a tear rolled down Polly's cheek, I hugged and kissed them. "Sorry. Sometimes you creep up on us, but that's exactly why we love you so much."

Chloe took Polly's hand. "After we get Matt better, we'll try to explain it to you."

"Without dissembling?"

I hid my smile and relief. Billy was back with his favorite word. "Without dissembling."

"Well, then," Polly began, sounding exactly like Lord Peter at his most reasonable, "seeing that we've got lots of questions, we'd better get Matt fixed so you can answer them. Jimmy said that Matt had to be put in mud, so Billy and I will dig up lots of it. Then we can make a bonfire down by Oyster Creek 'xactly like Jimmy Bones says. Come on, Billy. We've work to do."

As the twins ran off, squabbling as usual, Lady Peter came into the room. "Did I really hear what I thought I heard?"

"Yes. As usual, the twins think they know everything." I looked at Matt. If anything, it seemed that his breathing was a little stronger, but his face was still as pale as his pillow. "Lady Peter, what are we going to do?"

"I don't know right now. Give him some of Jimmy's leaves in a tea and wait for Peter to get back from the work yard."

The twins, of course, didn't see any need to wait. They burst into the room, demanding action. "We've got our paint boxes already down at the creek," Polly told them with pride.

"And, we dug up tons of mud. Enough to cover him," Billy added.

I looked at the still figure of Matt. "Oh, Matt, what have we done to you?"

"The tide's going out," Billy interjected, as though this was important.

"We need help for the bonfire," Polly added. "Thad, you'll come, won't you?"

I looked at Lady Peter in anguish. "It seems too pagan, somehow. I want to talk to Dan."

"Billy," Lady Peter said. "Find Preacher Dan and ask him politely if he would come up here again." As the twins began scrambling out the door, she called them back. "Billy?

Polly? What have I told you about walking everywhere, not running off like babies?"

Babies was apparently the operative word, because the twins left the room walking sedately. I wouldn't have bet on them remaining like that—not with the work yards half a mile away. But, it showed progress. I walked across to Lady Peter who sat staring out the window. "What are you thinking?"

"I'm thinking there's more that goes on in this world than I'll ever know or understand. Jimmy sensed immediately that Matt is a miracle. You had to tell me what had happened. I'm a scientist, but my science can't explain everything. It doesn't help me understand how or why I'm here in the nineteenth century. Science didn't help me diagnose Matt. I want to hear what Dan thinks about it all as well."

"What about Chaplain Johnson? Why don't you ask him?" Chloe asked, seeming amused that her mother would seek the help of a convict preacher rather than the family's man of God.

"Oh, he'd run all the way to Sydney, and tell all kinds of stories," Lady Peter said simply. "I don't know how to explain Thad and you, much less Matt. The poor man has no imagination. However, he's a good chaplain and an excellent tutor."

At dusk, we set off from the House down the hill towards Oyster Creek. As usual, Billy and Polly ran ahead. However, there were no shrieks from them and no squabbling. Chloe walked close by her mother, and I walked along with Lord Peter. Behind us, Preacher Dan carried Matt as easily as he would a sack of feathers.

When we reached the mudflats, we found that Billy had dug an elongated hole, roughly the size of Matt in the mud. The mound of mud had dried somewhat, so Polly dumped buckets of water over it to keep it moist. While they might not know what was going to happen, the twins had done their best.

Preacher Dan put Matt into the shallow hole and gently helped the twins cover him with the mud. Matt's eyelids flickered a couple of times, and Chloe grabbed one of her mother's hands. Then while Lord Peter and Billy set the bonfire ablaze, I knelt beside Matt and explained, as best I could, what was going to happen. Once the mud plaster began drying, Chloe and her mother painted a resemblance of his King William's uniform on it, and I put my boater on his head and his school tie around his neck.

Preacher Dan had stood aside while this was going on. I knew he had doubts about the "pagan-ness" of the process, but Lady Peter had told him that using mud-baths was an ancient medical practice, and surely he had to believe that God had made the mud. Once I finished knotting the tie, he stepped forward.

Silhouetted by the fire's light, he was imposing and I knew, no matter what happened, I'd never forget the sight. Vestiges of sunlight shone red against dark clouds. Mullets jumped out in the bay in their search for flies, and a mopoke owl settled onto a branch in a eucalyptus tree and began cleaning its feathers. Looking like muddy angels, Billy and Polly sat on the ground in front of their parents. Lord Peter seemed uncomfortable, and I knew he'd much rather be in his library with a glass of port.

When Dan began, he seemed to speak with the authority of God. He quoted scripture, and his voice waxed strongly as he encouraged Matt to be strong in his Lord and His power to fight against evil. He should put on the full armor of God, because he didn't fight against flesh and blood or the ills of this world, but against the dark powers.

I'd never thought of Dan as a warrior before. In the

faraway days of Greenway Hospital, when Gran read Harry Potter to me, she'd stressed that Harry's world was fiction and I accepted that. I hadn't questioned that Hogwarts professors would teach dark arts defense. Of course, they would. It was normal and necessary in Harry's world.

Now I understood how Christian the world I'd grown up in was. Lord Peter's strong Anglican faith governed Wahmurra in the 1830s. That was why everyone began each day with prayers. With this background, the Anglicanism of King William's had seemed natural. I was much more comfortable with compulsory chapel and religious studies than Chloe, because God had always been central to my way of life.

As I listened to Dan, I suddenly realized that people taught defenses against the dark forces in both my worlds. They weren't Hogwarts professors, and they didn't teach magic spells. Instead, they were folk like Preacher Dan and Chaplain Thomas at King William's. Instead of invoking spells, they prayed. It seemed so right when Lord Peter cleared his throat and began saying the Lord's Prayer. It wasn't Jimmy Bones's dancing and chanting. Nothing so dramatic, yet it felt so very right.

"Our Father, who art in heaven," Lord Peter intoned in his English upper class accent, and everyone joined in and stressed the "deliver us from evil" phrase. Preacher Dan followed this by reciting Psalm 23, reminding Matt that he should not fear evil in the valley of the shadow of death.

After a short silence, Lady Peter murmured to the twins that it was past their bedtime. Billy begged to stay so that they could keep praying for Matt. I kept thinking of Harry Potter. Harry had been able to put a real face on his evil foe. He'd been able to fight Voldemort physically. I'd give anything to be by Matt's side in death's shadowy valley with a sword in my hand. Illogically and although I knew prayer was my best weapon, I longed to slay Matt's dragons. But instead of a sword, all I had was my faith that God answered prayers.

I had to do something. To give myself a sense of helping, I began singing a hymn I'd learned at King William's for the Anzac Day remembrance service. "Fight the good fight," I started. After a startled moment, Chloe and her mother joined in. My memory petered out halfway through the second verse, so I just hummed the rest of it.

"Sing it again, Thad. I've never heard it," urged Dan.

No wonder. It wouldn't be written for another twenty years or so, but that didn't matter now. This time, as I sang, the others joined in more strongly, and when we finished, the silence didn't seem so oppressive.

"Look," Polly said suddenly. "Matt's trying to wake up."

At first, I thought she'd imagined something. But as I stared, Matt's eyelids fluttered. I began singing again, more of a reflex than anything, and someone behind me muttered prayers. Then I glimpsed a slight movement in the trees beyond the fire. I stared at the spot and gradually detected Jimmy Bones and a couple of his men, stark naked except for white painted stripes on their faces and bodies. They vanished just as I was about to point them out, and I couldn't help wondering what they'd thought of our very Christian version of their ceremony.

Uncertain whether they were a figment of my imagination or not, I turned back to Matt just in time to see his eyes open. He looked around, the alarm in his eyes settling only when he saw me.

"Thad," he said weakly, "I've been to heaven. Where am I now? Hell?"

22

The moon lit the path back to the House. As we passed the Barracks, I heard officers singing in their mess hall, and I sensed the convicts in their huts several hundred yards away. Some would be playing cards or telling wild tales about adventures they might have had. Others, exhausted by their day's work, would be fast asleep.

Nurse had a hot bath waiting for Matt on the lawn outside the House. She cluck-clucked over the mud, muttering that she'd never get it off, not in a month of Sundays.

"She better be careful what she wishes for," Chloe whispered. "After what's gone on tonight, maybe a month of Sundays *is* possible."

I laughed and began helping Nurse with Matt. Lady Peter bustled away to the kitchen and came back with a cup of horrible smelling tea.

"I hope it tastes better than it smells," I told her as she lifted it to Matt's lips.

Matt gulped a few mouthfuls then, to everyone's incredulity, tried to push the cup away. Preacher Dan immediately thanked God, and the following "amens" were loud.

"What now?" Chloe asked after Matt fell asleep.

"Now?" Lady Peter answered, "I'm going to get

Matt to drink a little more of this, then Dan will carry him back to bed. Nurse, ask one of the maids to put a hot brick into his bed to warm it. Billy and Polly? There's no use hiding behind Dan. I can see you." She smiled as they sidled forward. "You've done well tonight, but it's time for bed. Chloe and Thad? You've an extra half hour."

"What about Matt?" I asked.

"I'm going to sit up with him for the next few hours, then Nurse will take over."

"We could do it," Chloe volunteered.

"Bed," her mother said firmly. "I don't want you two sick. Like I said, you've half an hour."

When I woke the next morning, I rushed to Matt's room and wasn't really surprised to see Lady Peter already there. "How is he?"

She turned to me, her smile was wide. "He's feverish. He's restless. He's irritable."

"And that makes you happy?"

"Of course. Today, I know how to treat him. Yesterday, I didn't. It mightn't look like it, but Matt's getting better. He's in a natural sleep. He's still very weak and has a lot of healing to do, and I want you to sit with him as much as possible today. He's beginning to wake up and he's puzzled by what he sees. Sooner or later, he's going to start asking questions, and seeing you will settle him down. Now, do you know how to sponge him?"

"I think so," I told her, wondering how difficult it could be.

"Well, I'll have breakfast and then rest. Come and get me if you need me."

I was eating lunch when Matt opened his eyes. He stared at me, then looked around his bedroom. After closing his eyes and blinking several times, as though to make sure he wasn't still asleep, he asked, "Where am I?"

"Wahmurra."

He looked around the room again. "How did I get here? Where's Mom?"

I looked around the room too. I wasn't looking for anything in particular, I just didn't want to meet Matt's eyes. "Don't know," I said eventually. "We haven't been able to contact her."

Matt struggled to sit up. After I propped him against the pillows, he stared at my clothes and re-examined the room. "Is this a movie set or something?"

I laughed and stuffed the last remnants of my pie into his mouth. "Not really. It just looks like one."

The answer seemed to work. Matt closed his eyes and drifted off to sleep again. Chloe came in looking troubled. "Preacher Dan sent a message. He wants to talk to us after dinner. He'll meet us on the wharf."

"The wharf? Why? He never goes there."

"Don't know. What you do you think he wants to talk about?"

"Last night, I suspect," I answered, hoping she wouldn't detect my uneasiness.

Chloe grimaced, and I knew she wanted to talk about the previous night as little as I did. "Anyway," she went on, "Mum says to get some rest. I'm to stay with Matt."

Preacher Dan was waiting when we walked down to the wharf. His face looked worried, and after greeting us, he climbed down to the sand and started walking along the shoreline towards Oyster Creek. Eventually he stopped, and after looking around, settled himself onto a rock. "All right. I don't think anyone can hear us here, so plop yourselves down."

After we sat, he looked at us, much like Lady Peter did when the twins were in trouble. "What's going on?" he asked eventually. "That's what I want to know. And you, young Thad, can start with telling me, your best friend here at Wahmurra, how come you suddenly disappeared. Lord Peter said you'd gone to school in Sydney. But now, three years later, you're back with iron stuff on your teeth and not looking a day older. And, with her," he finished, nodding towards Chloe.

"Dan." I reached across and hugged him hard. He felt so solid and rock-steady. "I've missed you, but there was no way to let you know where I was or how I was doing."

"What's the matter with His Majesty's postal service? Why didn't you ask Lord or Lady Peter to give me a note?"

I understood why he was angry. I would have been as well if the situation were reversed. Chloe moved so that we became a triangle. "Dan, honestly, he did think about you. We both did. We talked about you and Wahmurra a lot."

"Then," Dan said, sounding hurt and sad, "why didn't you let me know?"

"Dan, neither of us understands what happens or why we seem to be the only ones, other than Lady Peter, who can do it." I went on trying to explain the inexplicable, using stars rather than time-gates.

He nodded. "I suppose that could happen. After all, Jesus left heaven and came to earth, didn't he?" He looked up at the stars and added, "All right. I'll accept that for the moment. But Matt? How does he fit into this?"

I took time, trying to sort my explanation out. Too much time, obviously, for Chloe because she jumped right in, explaining Jonesy, his antagonism to me, and the race.

"How far?" Dan asked.

"About three miles," I told him. "I'd rowed it a couple of times and found a current, like the one off Oyster Creek. Not nearly as strong though."

"It looked like Thad was going to win," Chloe chimed in. "It looks like he's using hardly any energy, and everyone else is rowing like crazy. Jonesy's about fifty yards behind, then, suddenly, a little girl falls into the river…"

"You'll never guess who it was, Dan. Not in a million years," I interrupted. I couldn't wait to see Dan's face when he heard.

"Well, if I can't guess, just tell me. Who was it?"

"Ol' Bundy's great-great-great granddaughter."

I got the reaction I wanted. "Are you telling me you rescued a descendant of Ol' Bundy? You, Thad?"

Chloe was determined not to be shut out of the conversation. "Yes. It was so awesome. Suddenly, Thad turns around, starts rowing backwards, then he dives under the water, and rescues her. Everyone goes crazy. Jonesy finishes the race and gets the prize. But everyone cheered for Thad."

"That's why I don't understand why he was so angry. He won. I didn't even finish," I told Dan, and when Dan started to speak, I put my hand up to stop him. "Let me get it all out."

Instead of continuing though, I started throwing bits of the seaweed into the water. It sounds silly, but throwing helped me talk about things I truly didn't understand.

"There was a party that night, and I think Jonesy was so angry that he wanted to get back at me. He put a drug in my drink, thinking I'd do something stupid."

"Drug?" Dan questioned.

"Think laudanum," I told him, referring to the opium drug that was common in the nineteenth century. "You know people get hallucinations from it. Chloe's world has a lot of drugs. People take them so they won't feel pain, or unhappy, or if they want to forget everything. Just like people take laudanum."

"That's bad," Dan said, sounding very preachy, although his face looked puzzled and I wondered if he knew what Chloe was talking about.

"Matt drank it instead of Thad, and his body reacted like it would to a poison. The doctors couldn't save him. He died."

"That I know," Dan answered grimly. "Jimmy Bones told me."

A silence stretched. Chloe had her arms around her knees; I filled in some holes in the sand and made new ones. Dan sat in thought. He was angry, I realized. I wasn't surprised when he exploded. "So, you are telling me that young Matt died because some rower won a race?"

Thad nodded. "Yes, and I don't understand why. Jonesy got really angry with me."

Dan rumpled my hair. "I guess that's because you took his glory away from him."

"But he won. He got the prize."

"And you saved a child. There's the true glory."

I shook my head. I felt I'd never understand. "I only did what anyone else would do."

"Anyone but Jonesy," Chloe commented.

Dan looked at Chloe with respect. "Ah, there's the nub of it. He, Jonesy that is, didn't do the right thing. He must have wanted to win that race very badly."

Only the quiet washing of little waves on the sand disturbed our silence for a few moments, until Dan continued softly, "Now, I think I know why you felt responsible for Matt's death. Why did you bring him here, though?"

"It was his only chance," I burst out, and went on to explain how we always arrived earlier when we switched worlds. "I thought if we could get him here, he mightn't be dead because it's still April and the race happened in May.

When we go back, it will be before the race, and things will be different."

"We hope," Chloe said, sounding pessimistic.

"Jimmy Bones knew he'd died, you know," Dan said quietly. "I don't know how he knew. I don't understand him or his world. Yours is easier for me, somehow. But, Thad, you've got to think about this. I don't know why you and Chloe are allowed this gift of changing stars, or whatever you call it."

"Time," I said softly. "Somehow we change time."

"Well, I've never heard anything like it. Jimmy might know about such things. I don't, that's for sure. But the thing is, Thad, you can't use it to play God. You're not in charge of the universe. You can't decide to resurrect people by bringing them back here. If that was what God wanted, He would have told us."

"We weren't trying to play God," I retorted.

"Thad, think. Out of all the people who died that night, you chose to save Matt."

"Because it should have been me," I snapped.

Dan shook his head. "You don't understand why I'm so upset, do you? Thad, what are you going to do the next time? Maybe, it mightn't be someone you love as much as Matt. It might even be Jonesy who dies. Would you try to make him live again, or would you let him stay dead?"

I shook my head. I did not want to have this conversation. "Stay dead, I suppose."

Preacher Dan reached across and turned my chin, so that I faced him. "Thad, do you really believe in God?"

"Yes."

"Do you believe in his grace and mercy?"

"Of course." Then I couldn't help rubbing it in. "You've talked about it enough times."

Dan looked surprised by my surliness. Nevertheless, he

went on. "Then, you realize that God's grace and mercy is for everyone. Not special friends. That's the difference, Thad. You saved Matt because you loved him. God offers salvation to everyone. That's the point. It's not just for friends. Do you understand?"

"No."

Chloe sat up. She reached for a stick and drew a semi-circle in the sand. "I think I do. It's the universal, not the particular. You're saying certain things belong to God because he can be universal. We can't. We pick and choose, like we would if Jonesy died," she pronounced, sounding very scientific and grown up. She thought for a few more moments before scratching out her sand circle. "Does this mean we're stuck here?"

Preacher Dan shrugged. "I don't know anything about that. That's for God to say. All I'm saying is that you can't use this travelling here as your private resurrection plan. There's a reason people die, though, I admit, sometimes, it's hard to understand."

I shook my head. "I thought I was doing the right thing that whole day. I never thought that saving Cindy Bundy would cause trouble. I thought I was doing the right thing for Matt, too."

"And that's why God allowed him to live, probably," Dan said. "Your heart was right. But it has to stop. The bringing bodies back and forth, I mean. Understand?"

We nodded and, after Dan got to his feet, he touched our heads gently. Chloe didn't want to talk, and neither did I. We just sat on the beach until the incoming tide forced us back to the House.

The next morning, Matt demanded answers and wouldn't be distracted. After Lady Peter nodded her head, I told him the truth about me. That I was really a convict. Then Chloe helped and we repeated much of our conversation with Dan, using the term "parallel universes" rather than stars. Matt listened intently before slumping back against his pillows. He seemed disbelieving and astounded. But that wasn't all. He was as angry as Dan.

"Did you ever think I might have been better off where I was?" he demanded. "I think I was in heaven. It was wonderful, warm and bright, and somehow sweet."

He looked at the ceiling, and then his eyes burnt into mine. "You made me tumble out of there into a dark and very scary place. It was cold. I remember being frightened and yelling for help, asking God to rescue me." He punched his pillow and stared at Chloe and me. "I don't know if I appreciate this new life. If it wasn't for my mom, I don't think I'd bother to live," he told us, looking the picture of despair. "What's worse, even after all this, you don't even know if I'll ever see her again."

23

"You two have to do something about Matt," Lady Peter announced one afternoon.

Chloe stared at her mother. "What do you mean?"

"Make him want to do things. He's stuck in bed feeling sorry for himself. I would have thought he'd be champing at the bit, trying to get out and about."

I felt miserable. "He's blaming me. I don't think he likes me anymore."

"What can we do?" Chloe was always the more practical of the two of us.

"Get him to exercise. Get him down to Lady's Cove and see if he'll swim."

"I know what might work," I said as Billy and Polly came running along the verandah. "Hey! You two! Come here!"

Billy and Polly listened quietly for a few moments while I explained my idea, then Polly raced off. She came back almost immediately with a bunch of hastily picked flowers in her hand—pink grevillea, orange bottlebrush, and, a beautiful red rose.

When she held them up triumphantly, I muttered under my breath. Lady Peter took one fast look and stood up. "Polly? What have I told you about my roses?"

Polly stood her ground, her chin stuck out pugnaciously. "It's for Matt, Mama. It's a bribe."

As I could have predicted, Billy came over and stood by his sister. "We're going to ask him to judge our contest, Mama. Thad said you wanted him to come down to Lady's Cove."

Lady Peter nodded her head, and immediately the twins streaked towards Matt's room. We followed much more slowly. By the time we arrived, Polly had climbed onto Matt's bed and was talking a mile a minute. "So, you see, I need you. Thad always thinks Billy makes the best sandcastles, no matter how beautiful mine are. I need you." After smelling the rose, Polly handed her makeshift bouquet over to Matt with a trusting smile. "You'll come, won't you?"

I knew that Matt didn't have a little sister. It was obvious that he was charmed and couldn't resist her. He smiled, smelled his flowers, and when it seemed that he might try to get out of going down to Lady's Cove, Polly disarmed him with a simple "Please."

When I saw Matt struggling to get up, I grinned. "You'd better hurry. If Nurse knows you're thinking of judging sandcastle contests, she'll be here to dress you herself. She'll swaddle you up like a new born baby before you know it."

While Chloe went to change her clothes so that she could swim, I begged a picnic basket from Cook. When we came back, Matt, dressed in yet another pair of trousers that Mr. White had "donated," stood, holding onto a chair.

He looked at me. "I know I've been suckered into this, but Lady Peter's right. I'm here now. I can't do anything about it, so I might as well make the best of it. Let's go."

It was a strange procession down to the cove. Chloe, with a couple of towels slung around her neck carried the picnic basket, while I helped Matt down the rocky pathway.

The twins laughed and shouted at each other somewhere ahead of us. Matt seemed to find their high spirits infectious. He looked across at me. "I suppose I've been a fool. Sorry."

While Billy and Polly built their sandcastles, Chloe went into one of the caves and emerged in her nineteenth century underwear. When she saw Matt looking at her, she grinned. "What can I say? I'm scandalously underdressed for these times and overdressed for ours. If anyone but the family sees me, they'll have a conniption."

I watched Matt watching Chloe as she raced towards the water and then swam towards a platform someone had built about fifty yards offshore. I wasn't really surprised when Matt sat up and started unbuttoning his shirt. "Do you think I can make it?"

"No idea," I told him. "If you can't, Chloe's a champion lifesaver. She once rescued me when we were more than half a mile out in the bay. Have a go. It's pretty shallow for the first little bit, anyway. You can always put your feet down."

With Matt continuing to get stronger, Lady Peter joined us on the beach one afternoon. "I have bad news," she announced, and somehow I knew it wasn't really bad news, just something I'd dislike. "Lord Peter and I have decided you must begin to live as normal as possible. Otherwise Billy and Polly will start thinking every day's a holiday."

As I watched the twins industriously building more sandcastles safely out of earshot, I supposed Lady Peter might have a point.

Matt looked at Lady Peter. "You're not going to make Thad go back to being a convict, are you?"

"No, no. Thad, rest assured about this. You're a member of the household, now. No, our plan is less drastic, but I don't think any of you will like it much. Peter and I have decided that you should go onto the same schedule as the twins. That means you'll have morning prayers with the household. Then, after breakfast, you'll have lessons. We still haven't worked out what to tell Reverend Johnson. Goodness knows what he's going to think with two new pupils."

"Two?" Chloe questioned immediately. "Isn't Matt going to be tutored like the rest of us?"

Lady Peter smiled. "Yes, dear, *he* is, but you aren't. *You* are going to learn the intricacies of running a household as large as this. You can help me do the stocktaking and work out our yearly order to England. Peter has told me there's a ship leaving next week."

I laughed at the look on Chloe's face. "You see, Chloe, women know their place in this world."

When Lady Peter and Chloe both turned on me with thunderous looks on their faces, Matt intervened. "Lady Peter, could I tutor Thad in math instead of us going to the chaplain? He's useless at the moment, not even up to our prep school standard. We could sit somewhere so that the twins will know we're working."

"The library," Chloe suggested.

Lady Peter frowned. "Thad, I don't understand. Mr. Johnson used to say you were brilliant at mathematics."

"I was," Thad told her. "But they've changed the rules. It's not the same, and I don't understand it anymore."

"What about Latin and Greek, Thad? You can't tell me they've changed," Lady Peter answered.

"Well, there's modern Greek," Thad replied.

"He's brilliant at them, Lady Peter. He gets tutored by a professor from Macquarie in Greek, and takes Latin with the Year 12s." Matt's face showed his awe at these weird accomplishments.

"How about you, Matt?" she replied.

"I haven't learned them. I picked agriculture instead

of Latin. Seemed more useful."

"I'm sure it is. However, Reverend Johnson is a magnificent teacher. I don't want Thad to forget his languages, and it seems an ideal time for you to learn them. So, you can do mathematics in the morning, while he teaches Billy and Polly. In the afternoons, it's languages." With that, Lady Peter put the tea cups and plates into the basket and for me to carry to the kitchen.

As I stood to obey her, I looked back at Chloe and Matt. Chloe's face showed resignation. She had no chance of getting out of her housekeeping chores. Matt looked like he'd run into a brick wall. I totally understood. Life at Wahmurra was structured. Now, Lady Peter had made sure that we were as well. It would be prayers, mathematics, and languages until she decreed otherwise.

A couple of afternoons later, Chloe tracked Matt and me down as we stood in knee-deep water on either side of Lord Peter's rowboat. "Going or coming?" she asked.

"Going," I told her. "Cook wants some fish for dinner. Want to come?"

"Please," she answered and clambered into the boat. "Quick. Get going before Mum remembers more things. I've been counting sheets all afternoon."

"Easy work. I've been reading Sallust," I retorted, referring to an early Roman historian.

"Sallust? What's he got to say about anything? He's ancient history. This is 1836, I think."

"Don't get him started on the ancients, Chloe. I've already lost that argument today," Matt said as he pushed the boat from shore and got in. "Mr. Compton's been earning nothing but praise all afternoon. I think we should throw him in once we're a long way out."

"My point was I've been laboring all afternoon," I said, trying to look stern. "How many sheets are there, anyway? It's not like there's hundreds."

"But there are, Thad. That's the point. Don't forget Mom has to order for the Double Bay house as well as here."

"So? What's so hard about sheets, anyway?"

"They aren't all the same. Some are threadbare and ready for cutting down into dusting cloths. Others are worn in the middle and need to be cut in half and sewn back together. Several need mending in other places, and others are all right. What Mum has to work out is how many new ones she'll need by this time next year, because it takes twelve months or so before the new supplies come. Six months for our order to get to England, six months for the order to get here."

Matt looked shocked. "I never realized the effect of the distance from England before."

Chloe nodded. "That's why we haven't seen much of Lord Peter. He's trying to work out what tools to buy, what machinery he needs. He hopes to get a new bull and a couple of horses from his brother to improve the stock as well. He's waiting for Mr. White to come back so that he knows what to get for the outlying farms."

Matt looked interested. "I can't imagine ordering everything from England. If we want to introduce a new bloodline for our cattle, we import frozen semen but that's not the..." He broke off as Chloe and I burst out laughing. "What's so funny?"

We kept laughing at Matt as I rowed us towards the Oyster Creek current. "Want to find out how I won both races against Jonesy, Matt? Look at the water, Matt. See anything different?"

Matt obediently scanned the bay. "The water's pretty calm today," he said eventually. "I'd say that the tide's coming in."

"That's good, country boy," Thad told him. "Now,

hang on."

On schedule, the boat bucked as it hit the current, then raced out towards the sea. "What on earth's happening?" Matt asked.

I explained about the current, and showed Matt how to get out of it by rowing across it. As we settled down to fish, Chloe seemed thoughtful. When she hadn't spoken for about five minutes, I asked what the matter was.

"Us. Mom said something today. She doesn't want Billy and Polly getting too attached to us, because it will be so hard on them when we go back. I think she's hinting so that I'll talk to you. We do have to go home you know."

"You and Matt do. I am home," Thad answered.

Matt put his fingers into the water and didn't say anything. After a couple of seconds Chloe faced me. "You can't say that anymore. Three years ago, yes. Now, no. For better or worse, you belong in my time. I'm sorry, Thad. Really sorry. It's twice now that I've messed with time, and both times it hasn't exactly worked out. You're still trying to make the twenty-first century work, and Matt can't figure out if he'd rather be dead. Well, I've learned my lesson, and I hope I don't have to pay for what I've done wrong. I do know that I'm through with pulling innocent, unsuspecting people through time with me."

Matt's line jerked and he reeled the fish in. We didn't say anything as we helped him kill it and put it into the basket. As it sat there, with its mouth open, I decided that was probably what I looked like as well.

Lady Peter was right, as usual. It really wasn't Billy and Polly getting adjusted to things—it was me. Although I stayed away from the convicts' quarters and the work yard, I'd begun to feel too much at home.

I couldn't stay at Wahmurra. I knew that. But it felt so good to be back where I didn't have to think before I said anything, and where I was loved and accepted. I felt like crying at the thought of returning to King William's. Instead, I faced Chloe. "When do you think we should go?"

"What do you think, Matt?"

By the time we tied the rowboat up and collected the basket full of fish, we'd decided on the following Sunday. If things went well, we'd be so busy at school when we went back that we wouldn't have time to miss Wahmurra. At least, that's what I hoped with all my heart.

The porridge at Sunday breakfast felt leaden. As I choked some down, I looked around the table. Billy and Polly were quiet for once. Lady Peter looked pale, and Lord Peter appeared worried.

"It was easier when we were little and really didn't understand that we might never see you again," Polly said.

"Much easier," Billy agreed.

We faced the equivalent of a reception line afterwards. Nurse, Mrs. Grant and Cook were by the door, all with tears running down their cheeks.

"Now, you be a good boy and make sure you don't disgrace us," Cook admonished Thad.

"You make sure that he behaves, Master Matt," Nurse instructed.

I felt the enormity of what I'd done. Once more, I was leaving my family behind. The first time I hadn't known about it, so I hadn't feared it. This time I did. No one in the twenty-first century cared about me like these two women. Certainly, there was no one who treated me like a well-loved four year old. Except, maybe, Gran at times. Chloe was fighting tears and I realized she had the same misgivings. After all, she was leaving her mother behind again.

All too soon we reached the Barracks. Preacher Dan guarded the entrance to the alcove under the stairs. After shaking hands with Matt and Chloe, he grabbed me into a bear hug. "You remember everything you've been taught, young Thad. Never forget that when everything seems dark, I'll be praying for you. And you too, Miss Chloe and young Matt."

Then it was time for Chloe's last hug from her mother, and big sloppy kisses from Billy and Polly. Lord Peter shook hands with Matt, rumpled my hair, and gently kissed Chloe. Wiping tears away, she stepped forward towards the yellow brick. "Matt, make sure you keep your arms around me. Thad, you're behind him. Hang on to each other and don't let go."

With my arms tight around Matt's waist, I watched Chloe press her thumb into the indentation my own thumb had made so many years before. She turned and looked at her mother. Then I heard a roaring sound and felt a wind like a tropical storm. I closed my eyes and felt vaguely reassured by the warmth of Matt's solid body.

When the noise and wind stopped, I opened my eyes and looked behind me. Billy's mouth was open. Polly had her thumb in her mouth. Lord and Lady Peter looked horrified, and Dan seemed to be praying.

"What's happening?" Matt asked.

I turned back to see what Chloe thought. She wasn't there. Matt's arms still stretched towards the wall, towards the yellow brick. But he stretched towards nothing, because Chloe had gone home.

ALONE.

24

Storming my way back to the House, I kicked every stone and pebble on the path. Why had Chloe gone without me? Or without Matt? After all, the whole purpose was to get Matt back before the dance. I remembered the saying "Be careful what you wish for" with bitterness. There had been so many times in Chloe's world when I'd wished myself back in convict Wahmurra. Now the wish had come true, words failed me.

Lunch was a somber affair. The twins were so quiet that I wondered if they might be sick. Probably, they felt a little like I did—devastated. As though Christmas had been permanently postponed. I excused myself from the table as soon as I decently could, hurried down to the wharf, and untied the rowboat.

It was nearing sunset when I rowed back. Matt waited patiently on the wharf. "Lady Peter sends her regards," he said, and I knew then how betrayed he felt.

"Sorry," I told him. "I needed to think."

"What about me?" Matt said, watching me tie the rowboat up without offering to help. "Didn't it occur to you that I desperately needed to talk with someone who might have a clue about what happened this morning? You brought me here to convict times, and I really don't know if I've forgiven you for that or not.

"Anyway," he kept on, grinding his toes in the sand, "I kept reminding myself that you thought you'd brought me here for my own good. I believed that, Thad. I even believed that going home was good, because I knew how horrible my death would be for Mom. I'd do anything so that she doesn't get hurt. I built all my hopes on going back with Chloe. But, what's happened? I'm alive, yes. But, in 1836."

For several moments, I stared at the two merchant ships in deep anchor, watching sailors swarm the ladders to light the ships' lamps. "I don't know what happened this morning. If you want the truth, I have no idea." I felt as old as the planking on the oldest ship. "Matt, I'm sorry. Sorry for everything. For thinking that I knew best when you died, for stranding us here where neither of us should be."

"And where I don't want to be," Matt added.

"Sorry," I said again, and then to Matt's surprise, I took off my shirt and waded cautiously into the water. I stared into for a moment, before quickly bending and coming up with something wriggling furiously in my shirt. "Supper," I told him, holding up a mullet that had swum into the shallows. "Tell you what. Rowing always helps me think. What say we ask Cookie for a basket and have a picnic on Too Far Island?"

"Too Far Island?"

I laughed for the first time since Chloe disappeared through the yellow brick. "One of my jobs used to be to amuse the twins. They always wanted to explore the island, but I told them it was too far. Next thing I knew, everyone was calling it Too Far Island." Matt smiled, and I felt relief. "Right. Will you tell Lady Peter what we're doing, while I beg food from Cookie? See you back here in five minutes."

I rowed us swiftly to the island. While Matt unpacked the basket, I scurried around finding twigs and wood and pulled a couple of stones onto the sand for a fireplace. When the fire began to burn furiously, I dragged Matt away from the beach. "Let's explore. It'll be a while until the fire burns down."

Matt frowned. "Aren't you going to cook the fish?"

"Of course. But, in the coals, like Jimmy Bones taught me."

"Tell me about him."

I climbed some rocks, then called back to Matt. "Sit up here. It's like a lookout. You can see the entrance to the harbor from here."

While Matt settled himself, I looked around. I'd forgotten the magnificence of Wahmurra's sunset. Although bits of the blue sky were still visible, the setting sun blazed scarlet and gold against black clouds, and their reflections smoldered in the water. "We're going to have fun going back," I told Matt.

"What do you mean?"

"You'll find out." I stared into the distance. "See that light across the bay. That's the Leamington's, Wahmurra's closest neighbor. Their house is maybe, four, five miles from here, but it sure looks closer. Of course, it's about forty miles by land. Strange, isn't it? That's the only light we can see from this side of the island. In your time, there's a whole city over there. That's where I worked during camps week."

When we climbed back down to the beach, I half-buried the mullet in the fire's coals and watched until its skin became a thick layer of charcoal. I turned it over, and when the other side was done, stripped the skin off. "Here you go," I said, offering pieces of the succulent fish to Matt. "It's not as good as Balmain Bugs, but we didn't pay a hundred dollars for it."

Cook had always had a soft spot for me, and the contents of her food basket proved it. She'd sent a huge meat pie, a couple of smaller peach pies, a container of trifle, and a couple of bottles of ginger beer. When Matt reached for one, I stopped him. "Careful with that. It's not the bland stuff you're used to. It's alcoholic. Some of the men make it down in the brewery."

"Wahmurra has a brewery?"

"Of course. Ordinary water's unsafe to drink in some places, so we use ginger beer or ale when we're away from the main homestead. In any case, some of the men wouldn't be happy unless they had their booze after work." I laughed when I saw Matt looking at the ginger beer as though he expected to see the devil's pitchfork on it. "Look. It's okay. It will only give you a little buzz, if that," I went on, and showed Matt how to remove the glass stopper.

It was hard to remember our problems. The water had stilled, and occasionally I heard a fish as it jumped for flies. Other than that, everything was silent.

"I never imagined that I'd enjoy a world without iPads," Matt said, breaking into my thoughts.

"I keep telling you. There's too much noise in your time," I said as he stretched and began packing up the remains of their feast. "Come on, get in the boat. I'll give you a tour of the island."

I rowed until we were below the lookout, then stopped, letting the night's peacefulness seep through me. "You asked about Jimmy Bones," I said after a while. "I don't know much about him. No one does except, maybe, Preacher Dan. Some of the men think he's a witch doctor. Others call him a medicine man."

"You seem to respect him," Matt said.

"So do Lady Peter and Dan," I answered quickly. "He knows things that no one else does. Like he knew about you being dead. Don't forget. He was the only one who had ideas about getting you better." I thought back to that strange night on the mudflats of Oyster Creek and shuddered. I never wanted another experience like that in my life. "Enough of that, though. The past is past. You can give me a hand rowing back."

Matt had been leaning back, his eyes closed, while his hands trailed in the water. He sat up hurriedly and when he reached for the oar, he screamed. "Oh, gosh, Thad. Look," he shouted, his face as pale as the early moonlight, and pointing to droplets of green as they dripped from his fingers. "I'm bleeding green blood. I must be dead after all."

25

I laughed and scooped up a handful of water and flung it at Matt. When Matt scrambled back in terror, I stretched my hand out. "Relax. Look. No blood. It's phosphorus in the water, Matt. There's nothing wrong. Nothing sinister. You're still alive."

Matt reached down into the water again, and when the sparkling green droplets fell, settled back on the seat beside me. "I've never seen anything like it. It spooked me."

"No kidding, country boy. Well, after what you've been through, I suppose that's natural." I took the left oar and looked at him. "You're right handed? You should be okay on this side then."

About one hundred yards from the island, I knew something was wrong. It seemed Matt needed two strokes to keep up with my one. I stopped and demonstrated, and although Matt tried, nothing changed.

"My right arm seems useless. Don't know what's wrong with it. How do we change sides?"

"Carefully," Thad replied, standing up to let Matt slide over.

The change helped. Matt's left arm was obviously stronger than his right, and once I throttled down my power, we managed to steer a straight course for the Wahmurra wharf. While I carried the picnic basket ashore, Matt tied the boat up. "I don't know what's the matter with my arm," he muttered as we walked back to the House. "I must have hurt it somehow."

"Ask Lady Peter to look at it tomorrow. I'll go with you. I want to talk to her about this morning. I'm so sorry, Matt. I thought it was foolproof. I never thought of anything like this happening."

"How does it work anyway?"

I shrugged. "I've no idea. I don't understand anything. At first, it seemed simple. Chloe put her finger in the brick's thumbprint and somehow we switched centuries. Remember when I haunted the archives? Billy left letters for me in different places. They all said there were more time-gates where switching back and forth could happen. When you died, I remembered Billy writing about those other time-gates, so I searched and found a place in the chapel."

I stopped and sat on the bench near the top of the path. "Matt, I swear. I truly believed we could get here by touching the stained glass window and go back by using Chloe's brick. I never, ever, imagined that we'd be stuck here. The worst scenario was that you'd stay dead."

"Maybe, I should have. All this trouble wouldn't have happened then," Matt answered.

"Don't be stupid."

Lady Peter, when appealed to after breakfast, could offer no explanations or even advice. "I understand it the least of all," she told Matt. "For me, everything changed when I touched the top of a pew in the old church."

"What old church?" Matt asked.

"He doesn't know, because he's never been to Wahmurra in his time," I told her. "I was going to ask him for a week in the holidays, but this happened."

"Matt, Preacher Dan is going to build a church for the convicts. I'm not sure whether or not he knows that yet, but it won't be finished until 1845," Lady Peter explained as she poured herself another cup of tea. "So, my time-gate, if that's what you call it, won't be built for at least nine more years. I accept that I can never go back to my old life, even if I wanted to. I know I might never see Chloe again, and that makes me sad."

That was obvious from her face. She dabbed her eyes a couple of times and sipped her tea before she continued, "However, I'm very grateful for what I have here—my husband, the children, and enough medical challenges for a lifetime." She put her cup gently on its saucer and stood up. "I can't mope around wishing things were different, that's for sure. So, I keep myself as busy as I'm going to make you. You'll stick to the timetable we've begun—prayers, breakfast, lessons, lunch, lessons, free time. Understand?"

"Lady Peter, can I ask you about my arm?" Matt explained about its weakness, and nodded his head when she suggested finding some iron in the work yard.

"You can use it like weights," she told him. "Let's see if that makes any difference."

Matt nodded again, and as she turned to leave, I touched her arm—something I'd never have done as a convict. "Lady Peter, please. One more question. I feel so cooped up, and I'm used to roaming around Wahmurra. Do you think there's a chance I could ride old Glossy again?"

"Have patience, Thad. I have an idea. I'll let you know in a week or so."

I was too restless to have much patience. After Matt fell asleep at night, I began wandering the House and as much of the grounds as I could, touching everything and willing it to be a time-gate back to the twenty-first century. One night when I tiptoed back to my room, Matt waited for me.

"Where have you been?" His cheeks were flushed, and

the bar of iron he'd taken to carrying everywhere was in his right hand.

I beckoned to the door. "Outside, or we'll wake everyone."

He followed me to a bamboo chaise overlooking the bay. "So, what have you been up to? Where have you been?"

"Looking for a way back. What else do you think I'd be doing at this hour? I've been going places I can't get to in the day time. I even went into the officers' dining room, because that becomes the Wahmurra Bistro. I've been trying to find things that I've seen in both worlds."

"Why? I get the impression that you don't like my world very much. Why are you trying so hard to get back to it?" Matt asked while doing an arm curl.

That, of course, was the one question I didn't want to answer. I had just worked out that I really did want to go back. "To get you home."

"Why bother? I'm dead there," Matt retorted. His teeth shone in the moonlight as he went on in a teasing voice, "What's more, Thad, I think I could be quite happy here. Think about it. Maybe I'm still dead, and this is heaven."

"Don't be silly. It's definitely not heaven. This was where I was whipped after my leg had been broken. I was a convict here. I'd be a convict now, but for Chloe. Matt, you were angry when you found out you were alive and in a different world. Well, think about me. I'm the same. I had no idea Chloe would drag me into her world. I worked hard to fit into it. Now, I'm not part of Lord Peter's family, but I'm not convict either. I've lived in three different worlds now, and it seems that I don't belong in any."

Matt did a few more curls with his iron bar, then put his hand over his heart, "Ooh. That's sad. Come on, convict boy. Stop feeling sorry for yourself. Your exact situation might be tricky here, but everywhere I look I see people who love you. From Billy to the cook, to Preacher Dan and Lady Peter. For a nobody, you've garnered a lot of love."

Heave, pant, and a few more curls. Then he continued, "What's more, at school, people like you. Of course, the teachers do, because you're so smart. But the rest of us think you're okay as well. I've never seen Luke Morriset go out of his way for anyone else, as much as he has for you. And, I feel I've never had a friend like you before. Someone I can really talk to."

I ignored Matt's outstretched hand and sat in thought. "It's just that I feel so different. In one world, I'm this. In another, I'm that."

"Listen to me, Thad. If you want to talk differences, think of this. I'm dead in one world. So, no, I don't feel sorry for you. What's more, you might be poor here, but in mine world you're filthy rich. So rich that nobody has any idea what you're worth. Now, take my hand and get up!"

I smiled as Matt pulled me up from the lounger. "Thanks, but you forget Mr. White. I bet he knows what's in the Compton Trust to the very last penny."

Matt grinned. "Well, very last dollar for certain."

Matt had told the truth when he said that he enjoyed Wahmurra. He was a country boy and he loved roaming the property on horseback, finding how little agricultural life had changed. Of course, machines were everywhere in his time, but cows demanded to be milked at sunrise and sunset in any age.

Sometimes, he accompanied Lord Peter on his inspections of the various operations on Wahmurra. One day Lord Peter talked about the possibility of growing wheat on the inland parts of the estate, and when he brought the prospect up again, one night after dinner, Matt advised against it.

"You have too much rain," Matt told him as we sat by

the fireside in the library. "Wheat needs a drier climate. Otherwise, it gets rust."

"Rusty?" I asked, a little amused by the thought of rusting wheat.

"Not like that. It's a fungus. At the moment, it's wiping out wheat harvests in Africa."

Lady Peter looked interested. "I thought William Farrar solved wheat rust about seventy years from now. That's why he was on the old two dollar bill."

"He didn't really solve it," Matt told her. "He only developed a new variety of wheat that resisted the fungus."

"You're very knowledgeable, Matt," Lord Peter told him.

Matt nodded. "I did a project on him about three years ago. King William's takes agriculture seriously. Anyway, Lord Peter, you can't grow wheat for another sixty years or so. Even then, it might only be possible on the western boundary. So, don't waste energy on an experimental farm. If you want to do something different, and if you have someone who knows how to grow grape vines, why don't you start a tiny winery on that old farm near Ruah Creek?"

"And have our own private label?" Lord Peter smiled as he stood. "Good thinking, Matt. Maybe you'd like to ride out there with me some day and show me exactly where you see this vineyard. Now, though, you'll have to excuse me. Mr. White's sent a message that he'll be back in a few days. That means I have to make sure everything's organized for him."

The next day Lady Peter interrupted Matt and Thad during their mathematics session. "Boys, quickly. I've just heard from Sydney that we have twenty visitors arriving tomorrow. They were supposed to come in a couple of weeks but, obviously, something's changed. I think a message has been lost somewhere. I need your help."

Both of us smiled as we stood. "Anything that gets us out of lessons."

"Well, to start with, can you transfer yourselves to Thad's old hut?"

"We'll need about six blankets each, if this cold spell keeps on," Thad told her.

"Get them from Mrs. Grant. Matt, you start and report back to me when you're finished." Lady Peter waited until he'd left and turned to me. "Thad, there's something you should know. We planned this house party long before you came here. Anyway it means that you'll have to keep out of sight more than ever. Mr. Semphill's coming."

I hoped I didn't look as stunned as I felt. I'd been assigned to Mr. Semphill as a convict laborer when I'd first arrived in Sydney. One day, when I'd been weeding the garden, I'd heard one of the maids cry for help. I'd grabbed a shovel, run into the study in my muddy boots, and threatened to smash the shovel against the head of the man holding the maid against the wall. Unfortunately, the man was not only one of Mr. Semphill's friends, but a member of the Governor's Council. He'd wanted me arrested and charged with assault. Mr. Semphill had refused, but he had not been pleased. There was no doubt that he'd remember me if he saw me again.

"What would happen? Would he take me back to Sydney?"

"I think the worst that could happen is that he'd ask questions that we can't answer."

"And won't stop until he gets an explanation," I said, feeling even more sorry for myself. I was scared of Mr. Semphill.

"They'll only be here for ten days," Lady Peter added. "But, cheer up. I have good news, as well. Peter and I have decided that if nothing changes, we'll send you both down to King William's as soon as they leave."

"So, that's Lady Peter's good news. School," I told Matt as he dumped his load of blankets on the floor of the convict hut.

"I hadn't realized King William's was even in existence," Matt replied, wrestling with a sheet. "But I suppose it's started up by now."

"It's ten years old, I think. We'll have to be really careful and behave ourselves. Haven't you seen the old flogging stool in the museum?"

I helped Matt make our beds. In 1833, the hut had been my pride and joy. I'd scrounged building materials and walked the beaches looking for driftwood. Now I couldn't stop myself comparing it to our luxurious bedroom at King William's. "I tell you one thing that's changed. I've become used to good thick mattresses. Our backs are going to ache like crazy in the morning."

Judging by the disgusted look Matt gave the makeshift beds, he felt the same way. "Might be easier if we slept on the floor," he suggested, putting his clothes in a neat pile and my boater on a peg. "What are you laughing at?" he asked, after looking back and seeing my face.

My grin grew larger. "I'm thinking about revenge, about getting even."

"Getting even on me? What on earth for?"

"Mathematics lessons. Haven't you realized? If we go to King William's, I'll be the mathematical genius again, and you'll be the dunce. No one will have any idea what you're on about. How does that saying go? What goes around, comes around?"

"Oh no." Matt's face reflected his dismay. "Well Thaddeus Compton, if that's so, I'm going to get serious, and pray morning, noon and night that we find a way back. You teaching me math? Ridiculous." He threw a pillow at me to emphasize his disgust.

Lady Peter's visitors arrived by boat the next morning. They were the cream of Sydney's society—the Kings, the Macarthurs, the Semphills and the like. After a quick look at their fashionable clothes and artificially high voices, Matt and I voted to eat in the kitchen. Lady Peter restricted our territory even further by putting even Lady's Cove off limits.

"There's only one good thing about all this," I grumbled as we fished from the wharf.

"This? Do you mean fishing from the wharf? The nobs from Sydney? Or, conceivably, being stuck in time?"

"I meant having to stay away from the visitors."

"And that is?"

"We don't have to talk like sopranos."

"Or with English accents," Matt added in his best falsetto.

26

A couple of nights later, well after dinner, there was a knock on the door of the hut. When I answered it, I saw Dan in his work clothes and, behind him, Jimmy Bones.

Jimmy had obviously made an attempt to look "respectable." He wore a pair of elegant pants, similar to what Lord Peter might wear in Sydney. They had been white once, but time and grime made them a speckled grey. Jimmy's cream shirt might have been one of Lady Peter's blouses, and he'd draped a rain-soaked red blanket over his shoulders.

It was Matt's first look at the man who had known, after one glance, what had happened to him. As I watched, I saw his curiosity fade to something like respect. We stood in an awkward silence, the rain thudding overhead on the corrugated tin roof, until I indicated the beds and pushed the solitary chair towards Jimmy.

Jimmy ignored the chair. He looked at Dan. "Tell," he commanded.

Dan cleared his throat. "Jimmy's upset because you're here."

"Only because there's so many visitors," I protested, looking around the poorly constructed hut. I still felt proud of it.

"No, Thad," Preacher Dan said. "He's not upset about the hut. It's you two. He doesn't think you belong at Wahmurra."

"Go home," Jimmy interrupted Dan's careful speech. "You no belonga here." He took a fast, curious look at Matt. "You dead boy."

I wanted to laugh, especially at the look on Matt's face, but I knew from the effort Jimmy had made with his clothes that he was very serious. "We tried to go. It didn't work," I told him.

"You not ready," Jimmy replied, taking a longer look at Matt but talking to me. "You get ready and go. Take him alonga you," he finished, pointing at Matt.

I looked at Preacher Dan. "Tell him we tried."

"I have. He keeps saying that the problem is you. I don't understand any more than that," Dan answered. After noticing that Jimmy was edging towards the door, he put his hat on his head. "Guess we're ready to go."

Jimmy opened the door. He paused and looked back, as though fascinated with Matt. "You good boy. Your god loves you." Then he turned to me, "You good boy too. You talk to your god but you no listen. You fix yourself up. Go home and take dead boy. Soon."

Half an hour later, Dan knocked on the door again. "I've seen Jimmy off. He's worried about you two. You're upsetting his world. Worse, he thinks you're getting too comfortable here. According to him, you don't belong."

"But what more can we do, Dan?" The words burst out, and my voice showed my frustration. "I've prayed. I've gone around everywhere touching stuff. Walls, pictures. Everything I can think of. I've even been in the Barracks' mess hall and dining room, and you know what would happen to me if I'd been caught. There's nothing, Dan. Nothing. Maybe Jimmy can work it out."

"Obviously, he thinks you should do it. There has to be a way, Thad. If there wasn't, Jimmy wouldn't have gone to all this bother. Put your thinking cap on. There's something wrong, and Jimmy's certain that you're the problem. Don't forget what he said about listening to God."

Long after Dan had left the second time, I thought about what Jimmy had said. "I might be the problem, Matt, but I have no idea what they are talking about. I don't feel guilty about anything, except you. I've told God, you, and everyone that I'm sorry about bringing you here. I don't know what else to do."

Matt settled into his bed and, shivering, pulled the blankets up. "Well," he began, "you can stop pouting for one thing. Whatever the problem is, it's not going to pop into your mind once you've decided to think about it. I'm just glad it's not my problem. You heard Jimmy. According to him, I'm just a dead boy." He laughed as he ducked my well-aimed pillow.

After breakfast the next morning, Matt scowled. "I'm bored. Let's do something different, something fun in our lesson time. How about trying to multiply using only the Roman system? Don't forget, there's no zeros. How about 459 by 36? First to finish sets the next puzzle."

We were trying to work out the height of the flagpole by only using Egyptian numbers, when Matt put his finger to his mouth. "Listen."

I listened.

Matt went on. "Is that what I think it is?"

There was the sound of a distinct thwack, and I looked at Matt curiously. "Cricket? I heard Mrs. Grant say that the officers have challenged the visitors to a game."

Matt looked like he had just heard angels playing their harps. Or trumpets. Or, whatever angels played. "Can we get on a team? Please, Thad. I haven't played in so long."

Matt captained King William's junior team. I knew he was a brilliant cricketer, I just hadn't worked out that it meant so much to him. "*You* can ask. Don't forget, I'm not supposed to be seen."

While I watched from some bushes, Matt walked to the parade ground which had been made into a cricket oval, or more accurately, a cricket rectangle. As soon as he appeared, one of Lady Peter's visitors beckoned to him. "I'm Theobald," he announced loudly enough for Thad to hear. "Can you bowl?"

"Yes," Matt told him.

"Good show. Come on."

About half an hour later, Mr. Theobald called a stop. "Thank you for taking it easy on us, young Matt. Now, have a bat yourself."

After the practice finished, Matt walked down towards the wharf so slowly that I easily caught up with him. I was about to tease him until I noticed his face. "What's the matter? It looked like you were having a good time."

"I was," Matt muttered. "But, Thad, Mr. Theobald was wrong. I wasn't taking it easy on them. I was bowling as hard as I could. My arm's just not strong anymore."

"Looked pretty good to me."

Matt stopped halfway down the track. "I used to be faster than anybody. I was fast, Thad. Really fast." He walked a couple of steps more before stopping again, and when he spoke, he looked and sounded scared and creeped out. "Thad, do you think my arm started to decompose when I was dead, and that's why it's not as strong? Maybe some of the muscle has gone."

I had no idea what to say. Was this the price Matt had to pay for switching worlds? For coming back to life? "There's only two people who might be able to tell you. One's Lady Peter, and she's as busy as all get out with the

Sydney crowd. The other's Jimmy Bones. Take your pick."

As I predicted, Lady Peter was indeed busy with her visitors, and Matt had no chance to talk to her. Instead, he walked over to the gardeners' huts and came back with a long-handled scythe. "Come on," he told me, "you can help."

I followed him to the clearing outside the hut. He immediately began cutting the grass as close to the ground as possible. "Ugh," he said after a while, when he stood and straightened his back. "When exactly are lawn mowers invented anyway?"

"I've no idea," I told him. "What on earth are you doing? Planning to cut the grass everywhere, or just here?"

"Just here," Matt said, bending over again. "You can help though. Make sure you leave enough room for my run up and pace off twenty-two yards, will you? Then put three sticks there for a wicket. I'm making my own practice pitch."

"Aye, aye, captain," I told him and began taking long strides towards the far end of the clearing.

Once he'd set up his improvised pitch and scythed the five yards in front of the wicket, Matt began bowling every spare moment. After a while I got tired of watching and went in search of a spare bat. "Might as well have a go if you're going to keep going on like this."

It took a while, but soon I was belting Matt's bowling all over the clearing. "I don't understand it," he said in disgust as we searched the bushes for the ball. "I'm not used to being hit. 'Specially not by a beginner."

"That's because you need to put spin on your ball," an adult voice commented. When we looked around, one of Lady Peter's Sydney friends was standing in the clearing. "Sorry. Didn't mean to startle you. I'm Evan Godfrey," he added, shaking my hand.

I found the ball, and Mr. Godfrey walked back with

Matt. "Your grip is wrong," he told him. "Don't hold it like that. Put your fingers here instead. Now take a shorter run, but do everything else normally."

I saw the difference immediately. Matt's balls skittered all over the place and were almost unhittable. To Matt's obvious glee, three balls in a row hit the wicket.

"That's enough now," Mr. Godfrey declared after another ten minutes. "We want you doing that against the army, not wearing yourself out," He turned to me, "Now, you, young'un. Let's get some polish on your batting. You can start by holding your bat straighter for one thing."

And with that, he took his jacket off, took the ball from Matt and started bowling. Half an hour later, I could just hold my own. Mr. Godfrey taught me how to pick which balls I wanted to hit and how to defend the wicket. True, it wasn't as much fun as belting Matt's balls around the universe, but I felt more in control. It wasn't hit or miss anymore. I had learned to bide my time.

And, biding time was exactly what Matt and I were doing. I couldn't wait for the visitors to leave. He couldn't wait for the cricket match, and while I was grateful for the cricket tips, I really wanted to talk to Lord and Lady Peter. Maybe they would help understand what Jimmy Bones had said. Then I could take Matt home.

In the meantime, the visitors preoccupied everyone. After some said they wanted to see the Chinese tea gardens about twenty miles away, an all-day excursion was planned. Cook had Matt pounding dough and me rolling pastry all day. "I need three kitchens to keep up with them," she exclaimed. "They just don't realize how much work they make."

The next morning, after we loaded Cook's baskets and bundles of food onto wagons for the trek to the tea gardens, she handed us two more packages. "Lady Peter says you should take the opportunity to go for a ride. If anyone sees you, they'll think you're two of the visitors. Go west, though."

I couldn't believe my ears. Finally, a chance to ride Glossy, and as we galloped towards the low hills behind the House, I shouted and shouted my joy. I'd half forgotten how good it felt to combine perfectly with a horse. "Tell you what, Matt," I gasped, after we pulled up for a breather. "No matter what world I'm in next, I am not going to go without horses. I love riding them too much."

Matt looked puzzled. "I thought rowing was your thing."

"Boats first, horses second."

When Matt suggested we stop for lunch, I smiled. "Let's keep going. I have a secret place not far from here. I think it's the most beautiful piece of earth there is."

Matt gasped when he saw my secret clearing. "It's incredible."

"And here's something you don't find in the King William's lunches," I called out, holding up a couple of bottle of ale. "Cookie certainly knows how to make our hearts sing."

Matt fumbled with the glass stopper before drinking thirstily. "Thanks."

"Again, take it easy," I warned. "Cookie sent it because Lady Peter would have my guts for garters if I let you drink unboiled creek water."

After he had eaten his fill, Matt lay back on the grass. In the leafy canopy above him, galahs and lorikeets made a tremendous din with their squabbling and squawking. Honeyeaters darted from bottle brush to bottle brush; wrens and pee-wees flitted around the tree ferns. From a gum tree branch, a Willie Wagtail greedily eyed the remains of our lunch, and every now and then, the sweet sound of a bellbird pierced the parrots' chatter.

Matt rolled his head. "You know, I don't think I've ever seen so many different birds."

"This is nothing," I scoffed. "If we were quiet and had the time, we'd probably see bower birds. Maybe, a lyrebird."

Matt laughed. "Thad, as I said before, if you told me that I could go without my iPad and be happy, I would not have believed you."

"And I keep telling you how noisy your world is."

Matt pulled a face. "Well, yours is as well. I can't even guess the decibel level of these cockatoos. And, at the homestead, if you go towards the work yards, there's the clanging sound the blacksmith makes when he pounds iron, and the windmill's clunking and clattering. Your world's pretty noisy as well."

"It might be," I acknowledged, "but at least you can get away from it."

"To here? Where you're deafened by birds?" Matt stared at the trees and their birds. He turned to me again. "Thad," he asked in a much quieter voice, "Will you tell me about the night I died?"

I grimaced. Did I really want to remember it? Still, Matt's question was valid. "Where do you want me to start? What do you remember?"

"I have a distinct memory of getting onto the bus, sitting by you, and saying that you'd be the only one the girls would want to dance with," Matt answered.

"Then?"

"Nothing. Just memories of heaven, I think. They're fading fast. I think they're becoming memories of memories," Matt said and then sighed. "What happened, Thad? Honestly. Not at the dance. Afterwards, I mean."

Once again Matt sighed as he thought back to that Saturday night. "Well, I was sitting in the common room watching TV when Luke came rushing in. He seemed relieved to see me. He sort of threw himself into a chair, told me the news about you and went charging off again to meet your mother. They sent a helicopter for her."

"Oh, my gosh," Matt whispered. "I've kind of ignored what she must have been through. Particularly when I died. Is she still grieving, Thad? Or, is everything kind of frozen until I get back?"

"I've no idea. Seriously. I really don't know how anything works. I know how it would be in science-fiction books, but this is different. It breaks the rules that everyone's thought up."

Matt nodded. "My dad's death was really hard on Mom. It was right in the middle of the drought, and he was doing everything he could to hold onto our place. Afterward, Mom sold most of our cattle at rock bottom prices. That was better than seeing them die of thirst. Then the drought kept on and on, and Mom got more and more tired. King William's was great. Dr. Rivers let her defer my fees. Then they gave me one of your scholarships. Eventually, just when it seemed we'd go under, the drought broke."

"Will you be all right now? Now, that the drought's broken, I mean?"

Matt frowned. "That's just it. There used to be the old ratio of five animals per square mile. Because of global warming, I think it's down to about 4.7, maybe even lower. There's a point where it's just not worth it. I feel bad. Our land's been in the family for donkey years. Since about 1875 anyway. It would be horrible to have to sell, but I wonder if it's worth hanging on when everything's so hard. That's why I think, if I'm really dead, Mom will truly break in two. She's been through too much."

"Then, you'd better pray that this plan of switching you

back in time works," I told him, pulling my knees tight to my chest. I was not enjoying memory lane. I was about to say something when I caught a flash of movement out of the corner of my eye. Thinking it might be an elusive lyrebird I turned and then scrambled to my feet when Jimmy Bones stalked into the clearing.

It was a different Jimmy Bones than I'd ever seen. He was naked, and I saw scars over his ribs from a ritual of some type. I didn't have time to speculate because Jimmy, followed by a couple of spear-toting men, stopped mere inches from my face. He stepped closer until I tottered on the bank of the creek unable to retreat any further.

He put his finger on my chest and pushed. "You no belonga here. You go home."

As he spoke, the men behind him lifted their spears to shoulder level. "I've looked everywhere, Jimmy," I tried to tell him.

Jimmy wasn't going to listen to excuses. He put his hand up. "No. Not true. You go home." He turned and looked at Matt, and I saw his eyes soften a little. "Dead boy! You help him! You know! You help!"

Another time I would have laughed at the look on Matt's face. Half-terror, half incredulity. "I don't know anything," he responded, his Adam's apple bobbing awkwardly.

"You think. You know, dead boy." Jimmy showed his yellowed teeth to Matt, in what I supposed was his version of a smile. When he turned back to me, he looked irritated. "You no belonga here," he told me once more. "Go home." With that and followed by his men, he marched to the bushes and disappeared into them.

I stalked back into the middle of the clearing and sat down defiantly. "How all the stupid, arrogant...."

"You'd better stop right there," Matt warned. "Maybe

he's just over there and we can't see him. Besides, I don't know. He spooks me. But, I think he might be right. I've been thinking about something for a day or so, trying to remember something you said about Jonesy. You saw him later, didn't you? I mean after I'd been brought back to the infirmary."

"Yes. Right after Luke left. Talk about broken people. You hadn't died yet, so he didn't know how bad it would get. But, he was sorry. He said he'd do anything to be able to do the whole thing over again. He wasn't talking about that night either. That was the really surprising bit about it. He apologized, not just for the drink business, but for everything else from the time he'd met me. And, do you know what? I believed him. I truly think he was sorry."

Matt watched in silence as I tidied away the remnants of our lunch. "Let's forget Jonesy," I said. "He's bad news. Come on. Let's get out of here before Jimmy decides to come back."

Matt ignored me. "Just a moment. "Listen. I've been thinking about this for a while. Have you ever thought you got it wrong?"

"Wrong?"

"Yes, wrong," Matt answered and slowly stood up. "Have you ever wondered why everyone thinks you did the wrong thing when you brought me here. I mean, I'm grateful and everything."

"What do you think I should have done? Let you stay dead?"

"No," Matt half-mumbled as he untied the horses. "I'd definitely rather be alive, thank you. But what if it wasn't me you were supposed to save? That, instead, it was Jonesy."

27

"Rubbish. Absolute rubbish," I told him and swung onto Glossy. "Rubbish, garbage, excrement, whatever. Still, rubbish."

But as we rode towards the homestead, I couldn't shake the feeling that Matt had hit the nail on the head. Jimmy said Matt knew how to get home. I thought back to the night Matt had died. There had been genuine repentance in Jonesy's face. But what was I supposed to have done? How could I have saved him? Stormed the police station and broken him out?

I worried about the problem, going at it from one way in his mind to another. Jimmy scared me. What would happen if I couldn't find the way back? I kept hearing Preacher Dan chastising me for taking God's place and asking if I only wanted to save people I loved. He'd specifically asked about Jonesy.

Feeling put upon, I wheeled Glossy around once we reached the dusty track leading into the Wahmurra homestead proper. "I reckon we've got about an hour before the Sydney crowd can possibly get back from the tea gardens. Want to take a chance and go for a swim in Lady's Cove?"

"We're not supposed to," Matt said. "Besides, we haven't our shorts with us."

"They won't be back for a while. I guarantee it. Come on, we're dusty and a swim is better than being drenched with well water. Hurry up and stop fussing. We'll skinny dip."

As we lazed in the water, I felt a sense of peace. The first I'd had in some time. The setting sun was turning the water golden. Close by, a fish plopped back into the water. Beside me, Matt floated and let the waves toss him gently back and forth.

If I concentrated, I could even hear the excited, high-pitched sound of ladies' voices as they started to climb down to the cove.

No!

By the sudden splash besides me, I realized that Matt was already racing towards shore. "Wait up, Matt," I called softly, "We'll have to hide in the ladies' cave."

Matt gathered up his clothes on the beach and held them in front of him. "Won't they see us?"

"No, there's a second cave at the back of the main one. We can hide there. They won't be able to see us, and we won't be able to see them. Hurry."

We sprinted across the warm yellow sand. I stopped ten feet into the cave to let my eyes adjust, then, just as the first lady entered, I pointed towards a dark shadow at the back.

It was almost pitch dark in the second cave. Matt swore when he stubbed his toe on some rocks in the center of it. "What do you suppose these are?" he asked indignantly. "They seem in a circle."

I dropped to my knees and carefully felt around the rocks. "You're right. They're either something Billy and Polly have put here for some arcane reason, or they're something Jimmy Bones uses. I can't see anyone else lugging them into here."

Besides being dark, the cave was at least ten degrees colder than the first cave and, even after dressing ourselves, we shivered. "I wish they'd hurry," Matt whispered. "My teeth are chattering."

In the outer cave, the Sydney women began describing every moment of their adventure to the tea gardens in their shrill voices, seeming to elaborate over each and every detail until I thought I'd scream. To distract myself, I began feeling the walls of the cave before coming back to Matt. Then I stubbed my toe on something and came to a complete stop.

"Listen," Matt said with excitement in his voice. "Put your foot back where it was."

I carefully edged my foot forward. "Oh, no."

Matt's soft whisper sounded as loud as a choir singing the Hallelujah Chorus. "It's old Partridge sounding off about essay writing. This is our time-gate, isn't it, Thad?"

I felt like shouting. Instead, I grabbed Matt and hugged him. "If I touch just a tiny bit harder, I think we'll go back. So, do we want to go now, or should we say our good-byes?"

"Do we have choices? Will something happen, and it won't work if we go away?"

"The brick always seems to work with Chloe. Don't see why this shouldn't be the same."

Matt hesitated. "The cricket match is tomorrow. Could we go after that? I'd love to see if my spin bowling works in a real match. I don't want to wait till next October when the cricket season starts again."

I laughed like I hadn't in weeks. "You and your cricket. Okay, play your match if it means so much to you. In any case, I'd feel bad if Lord and Lady Peter didn't know what happened, and I'd like to have one last talk with them."

As we made plans, the cave didn't seem so cold. After the ladies came back from their swim, changed, and chattered their way back up the cliff, we crept cautiously from the cave, and ran for the hut to change our clothes for dinner.

Afterwards we helped Cook with the mounds of dishes from the dining room, then begged Mrs. Grant to ask Lord and Lady Peter if they'd come as soon as possible. While the visitors drank their after-dinner drinks and played cards, Lord Peter arrived with a plate of cheese and his glass of port, followed by Lady Peter. Sitting outside on chairs from the kitchen, I took the initiative. "We've found another way home in a different place. We plan to go after the cricket match, so if we miss dinner tomorrow night, you'll know we've succeeded."

Lord Peter looked astonished. "Another gate through to your world? I thought we already had too many."

Lady Peter laughed and took my hand. "I'm glad for you. It's the right thing, Thad. You don't belong here, anymore."

"It's my home."

"Was your home, and, according to my wife, will be when you go back," Lord Peter told me. "And Matt, you must be excited about returning to your own time."

Matt smiled. "Excited, yes, and very thankful that I'm going back in better condition than when I arrived."

I turned to Lord Peter, the man who had been the magistrate in charge of me when I'd been a convict. "Sir," I began slowly, wondering how to put things. "Mr. White, the Mr. White in Chloe's time, told me that you continued to pay my wages even after I left here."

Lord Peter waved his hand. "It's nothing, Thad. I merely thought that you'd need a grub stake to get you going in your new world. It's nothing, I assure you."

"But it is," I gulped. "It's enormous. It's huge. Matt says I'm the richest boy in Australia, because Billy kept paying into it as well. Mr. White tried to explain it to me. In the beginning, it just grew through compound interest. Gradually, the money got invested in various companies. Part of it now is used only for investment capital, and Mr. White has picked some winners. Anyway, I wanted you to know that your money is called the Compton Trust, and it does a lot of good. More than half the income is given away."

"To people like me," Matt chimed in. "I'm a Compton Scholar at King William's. Without it, I wouldn't be there. If you're where the money started, thank you."

"I'm grateful, as well. But, very scared as well."

Lord Peter put his wineglass on the slate floor, then pulled me up and hugged me. "Thad, always remember it was given to you as a gift of love. It's yours. You can squander all if you want to. But I hope you don't, and that you will always remember the family here who nurtured you."

I started to say that I'd never forget, but he brushed the words away. "If you want to please me, Thad, keep using the money to help others. You've had many different looks at life. You've even been in different worlds." He sat down again and put his arm around Lady Peter. "Always remember your early poverty, your convict years. Remember us. I trust you and I trust God. When the time comes, and you take control of that money, remember how it began. A pound for every month of a convict boy's work. If you remember that, you should be all right."

"Besides," Lady Peter told him, "Chloe will have a lot to say if you're not."

Lord Peter stood, saying that he had to get back to their guests. When Lady Peter also rose to her feet, Lord Peter surprised me by hugging me again. "Go with God, Thad. Always remember where you began."

Encouraged by this affection, I reached up and lightly kissed Lady Peter. "You're the closest thing I have to a mother now," I told her in a gruff-sounding voice. "Thank you for everything."

Matt roused me the next morning in what seemed to be early dawn. "Come on. Get up. It's the cricket match today."

"Go away," I groaned and tried to turn over. "Wake me when it's over."

"Get up," Matt commanded. "I need you to practice with."

I pulled the blankets over my head, only to jump up outraged when Matt tugged them off and poured cold water all over me.

That was war. I got up immediately and looked for something to punish him with. "Gosh, Matt. Are you insane? That water's like ice."

"Ice is solid," Matt said as he raced for the door. "See you in the kitchen."

As least the kitchen was warm, I thought sourly, watching Cook scurry around preparing the usual huge array of dishes—eggs, mushrooms and kidneys, kippers, sautéed veal chops, and mounds of toasts. Matt smiled angelically as he stirred the tub of porridge, and I briefly thought about upending it over him.

By ten o'clock everyone had breakfasted. While the ladies went off to collect their parasols, Lord Peter led the Sydney men to the parade ground. After taking their jackets off, Lord Peter's team threw crickets balls at each other to sharpen their fielding, while the officers practiced at the other end. Hidden by a couple of bushes, I realized that Matt was taking everything very seriously, even diving to the ground to catch low balls.

Caught up in watching Matt, I didn't see a collision. When I looked towards the center of the field, one of the officers and Mr. Theobald were on their backs with everyone around them. After a minute the officer slowly got to his feet, but Mr. Theobald clutched his ankle.

For a moment I couldn't work out what was going on. Then Lord Peter pulled Matt away from the main group and start talking to him. Whatever he said didn't appear to impress Matt, because he kept shaking his head. Finally, and with obvious reluctance, Matt walked over to my hiding place.

"They say you've got to play. It's either you or Billy, and Lord Peter wants to win."

"I can't play, Matt. What about Mr. Semphill? You know I'm not supposed to let him see me."

"Lord Peter says he'll take care of Mr. Semphill if there's trouble. He says he'll put you on the opposite side of the field, and we can still eat lunch in the kitchen. I think you'd better say yes, Thad. Billy won't be able to do anything."

"Where is Billy anyway? I would have expected him and Polly to be squealing and running around."

"They're in disgrace. Lady Peter says they have to do their lessons today, because they put salt in Mrs. Simpson's hot chocolate." Matt took a fast look back at the field. "Come on, Thad. Trust Lord Peter. He said he'll protect you."

Even though I was apprehensive, I was excited. The officers had pulled all the stops out to make it a great occasion. Convicts had scythed the grass, so that it was relatively short and smooth. A special place had been set up for spectators, and ropes placed around the perimeter of the playing area.

"We have some special rules at Wahmurra," Lord Peter informed us. "If we hit the ball beyond the boundary ropes to the east or west, it's two runs. It's too short to be four. However, if anyone hits the ball so hard that it drops to the beach or the water, we lose ten runs. So, watch yourselves, gentlemen. If you want to hit hard, hit it behind or in front of you. Oh, one more thing. If you manage to hit the top cannon ball, it's an automatic ten runs."

"Talk about *Alice in Wonderland*," Matt muttered.

I grinned, until I found myself with the responsibility of guarding the top cannon ball. It seemed so much smaller than its twenty-first century version, because it hadn't been painted and repainted.

Once the game began, sometimes I'd run flat out to stop the ball only to be called off if someone thought it might go over the boundary rope into the water. Matt's bowling was spectacular, and I couldn't tell if it was because his arm was getting stronger, or because he was excited by the thought of going home and seeing his mother. In any case, just before lunch time, Lord Peter's team of Sydney gentleman and two schoolboys had limited the British army to a mere sixty-three runs.

After lunch, it was our turn to bat. I was penciled in at eleventh, the position reserved for the absolute no-hopers. Lord Peter and Mr. Godfrey batted first, and I hoped the game would be long over before I was supposed to bat. But the officers had a fast bowler who limited Lord Peter to twenty runs and Mr. Godfrey to two. In a surprisingly short time Lord Peter came over to me.

"Sorry, to put the burden on winning on you like this," he said with his usual smile. "Young Matt's already made thirteen runs. Defend your wicket, keep your bat straight, and let Matt do the work. Whatever you do, don't run him out."

I tried. The officers, knowing I was the weak link, kept me on the defensive. Usually I just stepped forward and deadened the ball and made no attempt to score. As Matt fought savagely and brought the run total up, I heard Billy and Polly screaming support in the background. "Hit it, Matt. Smash it to smithereens," they shouted, no doubt overjoyed to be freed from the schoolroom.

During a break while the bowlers changed, Matt walked down the pitch. "This is the last over. We need three more runs. When I call, run as fast as you can."

That philosophy worked. Somewhat. But I found myself facing the bowler, knowing there was one more ball to come, and that the score was tied. I'd have one chance to be a hero. "Hit the cannon ball," Polly screamed from the sideline.

"Hit it to smithereens," Billy shouted, while others in the crowd called encouragement as well.

I glanced over to the cannon ball pyramid. It was so tempting. If I hit the top ball, it would be ten runs and a win. If I missed, and he ball went down to the water, my team would lose. It was that simple. I measured the distance with my eyes, then watched the bowler pace out his run, turn, and race towards me.

The ball, once delivered, seemed the size of a large melon. I lifted my bat, and hit the ball as hard as I could over the bowler's head. "Run," I yelled to Matt, and when we reached the opposite wicket, the crowd exploded with applause.

As we walked off the pitch, the officers congratulated us and our team slapped our backs. "I would have sworn you were going to try for the cannon ball," Lord Peter said.

Matt grinned. "Me, too. I thought what an easy chance to be a hero."

"Or an idiot," I countered. "I *was* tempted, but I knew we only needed one run. It wasn't worth the risk. The other way was. Even if I was caught, the worst that happened would be a tie. You and Lord Peter deserve the credit. Not me for making some kind of fluky shot."

After everyone else drifted away to get ready for dinner, Lord and Lady Peter stayed. "What now?" they asked.

I looked around for Billy and Polly. "Where are the twins? Should we say goodbye?"

"I sent them to look for Nurse. I thought it would be easier on everyone if we just announced that you'd gone. That is, if you do go." Lady Peter kissed our cheeks. "Now, I must go to entertain our guests. We'll miss you. Whatever you do, make sure you tell Chloe I love her. Look after her for me, Thad. Always. Good bye and God bless."

After we said goodbye and shook hands with Lord Peter, I led the way back to my old convict cabin. "I suppose we should tidy it up. Fold the blankets and the like."

We worked silently until the gong sounded for dinner. "That's it. Let's change into our school clothes. There shouldn't be anybody near Lady's Cove, so we should be all right."

As we walked down to the cove, I had the sense of being followed. Every now and then I looked around. "What's up?" Matt asked.

"Nothing. Just a feeling. It doesn't feel right not to say good-bye to the twins. Without Billy, you wouldn't be here."

We didn't have far to go to find them. They huddled at the top of the cliffs, their eyes bright with tears. "You're going away, aren't you? Polly asked.

I nodded, my heart breaking. This was probably the last time I'd see them.

"It's not good-bye for keeps, Thad," Billy whispered. "We'll find a way to go to your world. Somehow. Even if we have to wait till we're older."

We hugged each other and as I kissed the top of their heads, I couldn't help but wonder if what Billy said was possible. That I'd see them again. They stood, turned and waved, and Matt and I starting climbing down the cliff.

My heart thudded when we entered the cave. Again I had the feeling that someone was behind me, but when I looked I couldn't see anything. I let Matt go first and, just before I followed, I saw Jimmy Bones, spear in hand, about six feet away.

"Thad?" Matt called from the cave.

I turned and, as I reached the second cave, I put boater firmly on my head then stretched back for Matt. "Hold on tight," I said, bending down to touch the ring of stones. Whatever you do, don't let go."

I asked felt a sharp push, and the vortex enveloped us.

28

When my head stopped spinning, I looked around for Matt. Had everything worked? Was he alive?

I felt unbelievably happy when I saw him sitting on the floor of our King William's bedroom. "Are you all right?"

"Other than being delusional, I think so."

"What do you mean?"

Matt groaned and rested his head against his bed. "I suppose I'll have visions of Jimmy Bones calling me dead boy for the rest of my life and expect to see him here and there."

"What do you mean, Matt? Have you seen him? He was in the cave with us."

"I feel like I have to puke," Matt told me, seeming to forget about Jimmy. "You didn't tell me it was like this."

"It gets easier each time you do it. Anyway, it beats the alternative in your case."

Matt groaned again as he staggered to his feet and looked around. "Well, I know where we are. Our room at school. What I don't understand is when. How do we find out what day it is?"

"That's easy. Look at my piles of new clothes. It must be my first day here. See?" I broke off and could hardly contain my excitement. Most of my clothes from the school store were still on my bed. "Don't you see? It's worked. We've come back into March, two months before the party. Just like I said all along. We arrived before we left. It worked!"

Matt looked around. "If this is your first day, I shouldn't be here. I suppose I should go to class, or do you need a hand?" he questioned, hope in his voice.

I started stuffing underwear and socks into my top drawer and put my shirts on hangers. "You'd better get changed if you're thinking of going outside the room. You look like you've been caught in a whirlwind and travelled two hundred years."

"And you don't?" Matt said and grinned. "It's good to be back, although I'll always miss Wahmurra."

"Come for a week next holidays. You'll recognize a lot of it. It hasn't changed much over the years. But we needn't worry about that now. Just get changed."

While Matt was in the shower, my mobile rang. "Chloe?"

"You're back. I've been so worried. What on earth happened?"

As I brushed sand from Lady's Cove off my feet, I began changing into my new clothes. "Long story. Where are you?"

"Enderby. In the turning circle. Waiting for you. Dad called. He said he can't find you, that you're not in your room."

"Well, I am now. If he phones again, tell him I'll be about five minutes."

"Thad," Chloe's voice softened. "How's Matt? He must be all right, or you wouldn't sound so happy."

Matt saw me sitting on the floor when he came out of the shower. "What are you doing there?"

"Damn and blast. I'd forgotten about my leg until now. Guess my adrenaline was so high before, it didn't matter. But this is the day I got out of the infirmary. My leg hasn't healed yet. I'm back to needing crutches and I'd forgotten how much I hate them." I picked one up and wanted to hurl it through a window. "Drat it to blazes. My leg hurts and it's as feeble as one of Polly's excuses."

"Or my arm," Matt said. "It feels all right though. Have you seen my tie? Can you lend me one?"

I watched Matt knotted his borrowed tie and realized we'd just solved one of the mysteries. Billy must have kept Matt's tie and used it instead of string on the package he left in his bedroom. Before I could say anything, the end of lessons bell rang in the distance. As Matt scrambled into his jacket, I asked, "Do you remember what happens?"

Matt nodded. "Mom's down, and she's taking me out for the weekend."

"Starting with dinner at Michael Dee's? Listen, I just had a wacky idea. But your mum's lonely, and Chloe's dad is sort of on the rebound. What do you think?"

Matt took about five steps backwards and held his hands up in supposed horror. "I'm staying right away from your ideas. Now, are you ready?"

I reached for my crutches and scuffled out of the room. I'd just reached the outer door when it crashed open and a group of boys came through. One stopped.

It was Jonesy. He stood half a head taller than his friends and still had his glorious haircut. Once again I looked at his beautiful face marred with bitterness and thought that he looked like a fallen angel.

"Well, well, well," Jonesy said. "What have we here?"

He took a step towards me, seemed to hesitate for a moment then pushed my shoulders hard enough that I fell to the ground.

Again.

It should not have hurt. I'd been expecting it, but once again, I'd forgotten my weak leg. For several long seconds, I envisioned the satisfaction of punching the smug look from Jonesy's face. Only after Matt came and stood next to me did I pull myself together.

I remembered the many times Jonesy had shouldered me into lockers, and the pain from wet towels being slapped on my legs. I hadn't forgotten the drugged drink, or the look on Jonesy's face that horrible night when he'd wished for a chance to do things differently. Jimmy Bones had been right. Jonesy was the one I needed to save.

"Hi!" I said, twisting myself around to face him. *Please make this work*, I prayed as I turned on my best smile. "I'm Thad Compton, and I've just had surgery on my leg. Would you give me a hand up?"

Jonesy looked at me, his face frozen. I thought I detected a baffled look in his eyes, but I could have been mistaken.

His friends had no such hesitation. They hooted and hollered about me being the cripple Jonesy had had to change rooms for, and how they didn't need any more crips. Jonesy didn't move. He simply stood there, ignoring my outstretched hand, lost in thought. Then he shook his head. "I had the strangest dream about this."

He stared at me for several more long seconds. Gradually Kyle Beresford and Alton quietened, and we became a tableau. Then Jonesy shook his head, as though he was shaking his dream away.

He reached down and grabbed my hand. "I'm Bruce Jones. But never, if you value your life, call me Bruce. I'm Jonesy."

I saw the shock on Matt's face as Jonesy hauled me to my feet and started to walk away. Then he seemed to have second thoughts and came back. "Look, there's space in my cadet corps, right now."

Jonesy looked at me and, for a second, the old ugly smile appeared as he went on. "I realize you mightn't be able to do what the rest of us can, even when you're better."

NO. It wasn't going to be the same, was it?

Then Jonesy shook his head, like he was getting water out of his ears or something, and I thought he was genuine when he held his hand out and continued, "I'd be happy to show you around. So, do you want to sign up?"

ABOUT THE AUTHOR

Beverley Boissery was born in Sydney, Australia and now lives in Vancouver, Canada with her very long time (18 years) feline friend, Lillee. She has a Ph. D in history from The Australian National University and an insatiable curiosity about time and God.

Bev loves hearing from her readers. Visit her website –

http://beverleyboissery.com

Made in the USA
Charleston, SC
04 February 2014